BLAKE'S

NAPLAN Year 5 Test Guide

Merryn Whitfield & Lyn Baker

PASCAL PRESS

Blake's NAPLAN* Year 5 Test Guide

ISBN: 978 1 74215 943 0

Published by Pascal Press
PO Box 250
Glebe NSW 2037
www.pascalpress.com.au
contact@pascalpress.com.au

Authors: Merryn Whitfield & Lyn Baker
Publisher: Lynn Dickinson
Editor: Karen Jayne
Typesetter: Ruth Schultz
Design and illustration: Janice Bowles

CONTENTS

About the Authors v
Introduction vi
How to Use This Book vi

LITERACY 1
READING 4
Types of Text 4
Locating Information 6
Connecting Information 9
Making Inferences 11
Applied Comprehension 15
Visual Literacy 18
Sequencing 20
The Main Idea 23
Reasoning 24
Figurative Language 27
Reading Practice Test 31

WRITING 36
Persuasive Texts 37
Audience 39
Structure 40
Ideas 41
Persuasive Devices 42
Vocabulary 43
Cohesion 44
Paragraphs 45
Sentence Structure 46
Punctuation 47
Spelling 48
Planning a Persuasive Text 49

Narrative Texts 62
Audience 63
Structure 64
Ideas 66
Character & Setting 68
Vocabulary 69
Cohesion 70
Paragraphs 71
Sentence Structure 72
Punctuation 73
Spelling 74
Planning a Narrative Text 75

Informative Texts 90
Audience 91
Structure 92
Ideas 94
Description & Details 95
Vocabulary 97
Cohesion 98
Paragraphs 99
Sentence Structure 100
Punctuation 101
Spelling 102
Planning an Informative Text 103

CONTENTS continued...

LANGUAGE CONVENTIONS	117
Spelling	117
Grammar	127
Punctuation	135
Language Conventions Practice Test	**139**

NUMERACY	**142**
Checklists	**152**
Numbers and Place Value	152
Working with Numbers	153
Addition and Subtraction	154
Multiplication	155
Division	156
Fractions and Decimals	157
Money	158
Patterns	159
Measurement	160
Time	161
Perimeter, Area and Volume	162
Shapes	163
Objects	164
Location	165
Symmetry and Transformations	166
Angles	167
Chance	168
Data	169
Numeracy Practice Test	**170**

ANSWERS	177

ABOUT the AUTHORS

Merryn Whitfield is an experienced educator currently working as a teacher in a New South Wales primary school. Over the past two decades, she has taught students from diverse cultural and socio-economic backgrounds across all stages K–6. Merryn has undertaken various educator positions including Assistant Principal; 'Minds in Motion' presenter; SCAN reviewer; and has led several teacher in-service courses in writing, grammar and NAPLAN analysis and testing.

Merryn has consistently worked with educators in public schools providing professional support and expertise, while guiding and encouraging changed classroom methodology and improved literacy practices. She is the author of many educational materials, including the best-selling *Excel – Parent's Guide to Primary English and Mathematics; Blake's Writer's Guide; Maximising Test Results: Reading and Writing;* the award-winning *Targeting Writing Across the Curriculum* series; and the innovative CD rom series *Targeting Text Interactively*, and she has designed an extensive range of classroom resources for educators.

Her personal interests include her young family, water sports and reading widely.

Lyn Baker has been a teacher of mathematics for many years. She has written lots of books for students of all ages from year 2 to year 12. She has also written questions for the *Excel Test Zone* and for *Excel HSC Quick Study Apps.*

Lyn lives on a farm and enjoys looking after lots of animals.

INTRODUCTION

The National Assessment Program for Literacy and Numeracy (NAPLAN*) is a Federal Government initiative that requires the assessment of skills in literacy and numeracy across all Australian schools for students in years 3, 5, 7 and 9.

The literacy tests measure student performance in three sections:

1 Reading
2 Writing
3 Language conventions (including spelling, grammar and punctuation)

In the numeracy test you will find questions from the three strands of the curriculum. These are:

1 Number and Algebra
2 Measurement and Geometry
3 Statistics and Probability

The NAPLAN tests typically occur early in term two (May) of each year and are conducted over three days. All schools Australia wide must complete the tests on the same day.

Day 1 – Language conventions (40 minutes)
– Writing (40 minutes)
[5 minutes planning, 30 minutes writing, 5 minutes editing]

Day 2 – Reading (50 minutes)

Day 3 – Numeracy (50 minutes)

* This is not an officially endorsed publication of the NAPLAN program and is produced by Pascal Press independently of Australian Governments.

HOW TO USE THIS BOOK

Blake's NAPLAN Year 5 Test Guide provides you with the tools and strategies you will need to approach your NAPLAN tests with confidence. It will help you develop knowledge and understanding of the types of questions you may face and the best way to successfully approach them.

This user friendly guide contains:

- sections on each key aspect of the NAPLAN tests
- examples of different types of questions
- opportunities to practise strategies using the TRY THIS sections
- definitions of key terms in clear, concise and friendly language
- answers to the TRY THIS and Practice Tests sections.

Blake's NAPLAN Year 5 Test Guide is a vital reference for anyone wanting to successfully approach the NAPLAN tests with confidence and skill.

LITERACY

QUESTION TYPES

When you complete your NAPLAN tests, you will be asked to provide answers in several different ways.

Never leave a multiple choice question unanswered. Even if you guess – you might just get it right!

Multiple choice

The most common answer type is multiple choice. The good thing about multiple choice answers is that you know one of them MUST be correct.

When answering multiple choice questions in NAPLAN, it is important to fill in the bubble completely –

Like this: ⬬ ✓

NOT like this: ◯ ✗

What is the title of this book?

- ◯ Help me please!
- ⬬ Blake's NAPLAN Year 5 Test Guide
- ◯ I don't want to do NAPLAN
- ◯ Blake's Homework Helper

Some more tips for multiple choice questions:

- Skip any questions that seem too hard and come back to them at the end.
- Try to answer the question without looking at the choices. Then read through the choices. This allows you to make a clearer decision.
- Completely erase an incorrect answer before you change it.
- Look at the answers given. Are there any that are obviously wrong? You may have only two choices now and this will give you a better chance of choosing the correct answer.

Single word

In the spelling section of the language conventions test, you will be asked to write single word answers in a box like this:

If you make a mistake, erase the word COMPLETELY before writing the correct answer.

You must remember to make sure the whole word fits inside the box and does not go out.

Like this: testing ✓

Not this: testing ✗

Try this

What is the correct spelling of the underlined word?

Homework is the <u>werst</u> thing in the whole wide world!

Sequencing

In some NAPLAN tests, you will be asked to put events or objects in order. This is called sequencing.

When you answer sequencing questions, you MUST put a number in EACH BOX. If you miss a box, you will get the answer incorrect.

Write the numbers 1 to 4 in the boxes to show the order of events in an afternoon.

- [2] Have a sugar-filled snack
- [3] Tell your mum you don't have homework
- [1] Change out of your horrible school uniform
- [4] Watch television

Try this

Put these food items in order from the best to the worst.

- [ ] Broccoli
- [ ] Liver
- [ ] Banana
- [ ] Chocolate

Short answer

These types of questions ask you to provide an answer using several words or one or two sentences. The answer you give is written on lines, not in boxes.

A short answer is most often found in the reading test, and usually needs you to give your own opinion BASED ON what you have read in the text.

The Amazing Adventures of Booga Boy!

Just in time for the school holiday crowds, this movie is perfectly timed.

A creative and vibrant advertising campaign has made sure that Booga Boy and his gang are household names. Despite some frightening scenes, which will make the junior viewers run for cover, *The Amazing Adventures of Booga Boy* is not to be missed!

Rated: PG **Running Time:** 1 hr 35 mins **Rating:** ★★★★☆

Who would be the target audience for this movie review? Give a reason for your answer. Write your answer on the lines.

Its target audience would be primary school aged children, but not really young ones in kindergarten because they might get too scared.

School work is just dreadful,
Spelling is a pain.
Tomorrow is a fractions test,
That really hurts my brain!

How does the author feel about school? Give a reason for your answer.

____

____

____

Try this

Use words from the text to support your answer.

READING

INTRODUCTION

Don't read all the texts at once. It will get too confusing when you have to try to remember the details when answering the questions.

You will have up to 50 minutes to complete your NAPLAN reading test. There will be six different texts to read; but don't worry, none of them are over one page in length.

So what is the best way to start your NAPLAN reading test?

After you have completed the practice questions with your teacher, you will be allowed to begin.

1. Read the first text in your reading booklet.
2. Look at the questions on your test paper that match the text you have read.
3. Remember to go back to the text to confirm your answers.
4. Once you have answered all the questions for the first text, move on to the next one.

For each text, there will be 6–8 questions to be answered. These questions will test different aspects of reading comprehension. In this section of *Blake's NAPLAN Year 5 Test Guide*, you will have the chance to learn about and practise answering some of these question types.

TYPES OF TEXTS

Narrative	**Poem**
• Tells a story with a problem • Its main purpose is to entertain • Uses lots of description, action verbs, direct speech and figurative language • Can be written by a character in the story (1st person) or narrator outside of the events (3rd person)	• Can take many forms • Written in verses or stanzas • Can tell a story, or convey an image or emotion • Uses rhyme and rhythm as well as figurative language • Does not have to use complete sentences

Myth/Legend	Fable
• A type of narrative • Main purpose is to explain how things became the way they are • Presented as history, but unlikely to be true	• A type of narrative • Main purpose is to give a moral or message about the correct way to behave • Often uses animal characters
Report • Main purpose is to present information about something • Focuses on one topic or subject • Each paragraph provides details about a different feature • Uses lots of noun groups and descriptive language	**Review** • Main purpose is to persuade the reader to follow a course of action • Is a formal judgement on a film, book, performance • Contains some information, but relies on opinion
Procedure • Main purpose is to instruct HOW to do something • Formats include recipes, instructions or directions • Includes lists of materials and/or helpful hints • Uses commanding verbs	**Explanation** • Main purpose is to explain how or why something happens • Often related to natural or scientific events such as weather conditions or animal lifecycles • Uses technical vocabulary • Starts with a definition of the event or a question
Recount • A retelling of a series of events • Can be personal or historical • Can include facts and opinions • Uses time-based connectives and conjunctions	**Exposition** • Main purpose is to present opinions • Argument – one side of the issue • Discussion – two different opinions of the issue • Uses high modality (should, must, never) • Different arguments and reasons in separate paragraphs
Tables/Graphs • Visual ways to represent information • Uses images more than words • Readers often need to use background knowledge and inference	**Poster/Flyer** • Often a form of advertisement or promotion • A type of exposition • Uses images and key points with a minimum of reading

LOCATING INFORMATION

The Honeybee Dinner Dance

You have to be a good dancer to make it as a honeybee. Honeybees dance to send their messages. When a bee finds food, it flies back to the hive to dance. The type of dance tells the other bees where the food is.

If the food is far away, the bee's dance looks like a number eight. This dance is known as 'the waggle dance'. If the food is close to the hive, the bee dances in circles. And the more flowers there are with sweet, liquid nectar to feast on the faster the dance!

Why do honeybees dance?

- ○ They are trying out for reality TV
- ○ They can only count to 8
- ● To communicate with each other
- ○ They look silly when they waggle their bottoms

Look for the answer in the text. Sometimes the answer might use a word that is different to the text, but which has the same meaning. In this case messages = communicate

Honeybees dance quickly when:

- ○ they need to go to the toilet
- ○ they are hungry
- ○ they have had too much nectar to drink
- ● there is lots of food available

What you are being asked to do here is find FACTS and DETAILS. They usually involve questions such as:

Who? | What? | When? | Where? | How?

Try this

Whales

Whales come from the family known as cetaceans. Despite what many people think, they are not fish. In fact they are warm-blooded, air-breathing mammals. Most whales live in the icy waters of the Arctic and Antarctic and use their thick layers of fatty blubber to keep warm. There are two types of cetaceans – toothed and baleen.

Toothed Whales

Cetaceans such as dolphins are known as **odontocetes** and can have anywhere from 2–250 teeth. They use their teeth to grip their food such as squid and fish, rather than chew them. Their prey is located by using **echolocation**. The signals sent out from the front of their heads bounce off objects and return to the whale through their hollow lower jaw. Toothed whales live in large social groups, known as pods. Each pod usually contains one male with many females and their calves.

Baleen Whales

Unlike their toothed relations, baleen whales such as humpback whales have two blowholes, not just one. They also live in smaller family based groups and have only one mate. Instead of teeth, baleen whales have a series of plates, called whalebone. These plates are made of keratin, like our fingernails, and hang down from their upper jaw. They act like a sieve, straining out the food such as plankton and krill. Hence, they have been nicknamed 'filter feeders'. Baleen whales feed during the summer and then migrate to warmer waters to breed.

Whales (2002) [Online] www.kidcyber.com.au

What do toothed whales use their teeth for?

◯ Eating ◯ Chewing ◯ Smiling ◯ Holding

How are people and whales similar?

◯ We have body parts made of keratin ◯ We blubber when we cry

◯ We like to swim ◯ We use echolocation

How many teeth do baleen whales have?

◯ 2 ◯ none ◯ nobody knows ◯ up to 250

A New Day

Fresh, cool air flowed out of the vents and into the room. The metal plates covering the windows quietly rolled down. The new day's artificial light shone in and bounced off the metal walls. The sweet sounds of birds filtered through the speakers.

Tyson stirred and rolled over in the bed. He pulled the blanket over his head.

"Time to rise."

"Who or what was that?" thought Tyson as he peered over the top of the blanket. A robot stood at the end of his bed. Tyson closed his eyes tightly, and then opened them again. The robot was still there holding some clothes. They were clothes Tyson would never wear in a million years.

Tyson scanned the room. This wasn't his room. It was too clean and there was too much metal. Where were his posters? His basketball ring?

Why did Tyson pull the blanket up over his head?

- ○ He wanted to ignore the robots
- ● He was trying to block out the light and the noise
- ○ He was scared
- ○ He was lost

Look for what happens BEFORE the event, not after.

Try this

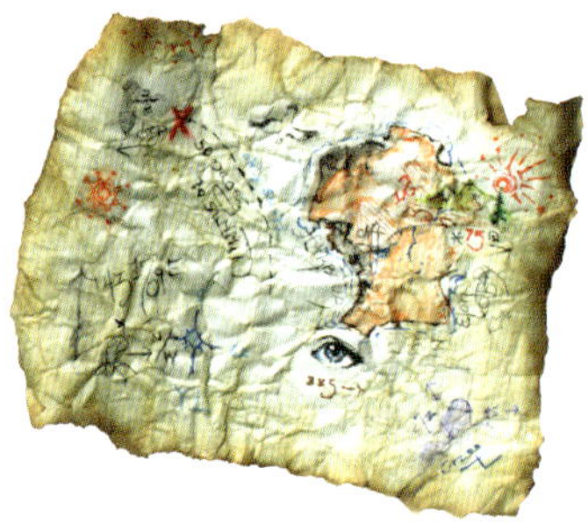

"Now go and clean up that pigsty!" shouted Mum.

"Aye! Aye! Captain," I grumbled. Scrubbing decks and making everything shipshape was not my idea of a pleasant Saturday afternoon.

Secretly I decided to continue my week-long search for the long lost treasure of Nobeard Bedhair, the fearsome pirate chief. Digging out the ancient map, torn and frayed, I located the last known position of the priceless artefact (a page of spelling homework) – three paces due north of Black Sands lagoon.

Before commencing the search, I made sure that the feisty captain was occupied below decks. Yes, there she was, hunched over the galley bench, muttering about the inaccurate log books and supply lists.

OK, the coast was clear.

Why does the author want to continue the search 'secretly'?

- ○ Pirates are scary
- ○ He doesn't want to share it with the captain
- ○ Treasure is always lost
- ○ Mum wants him to clean up instead

CONNECTING INFORMATION

Dear Rita,

I read with interest your ad in the local newspaper last week and my company, **Perfect Fur You**, is very interested in participating in the sponsorship program.

We believe that it is our duty to nurture and support other living creatures. We would be particularly interested in sponsoring an Australian endangered animal as they are far more appealing, don't you agree?

It is so sad to see on TV the devastating effect that modern development has had on our furry and feathered companions. That is the key motivation for us to take up the opportunity to play a small part in easing their suffering through your marvellous sponsorship program.

What is the main reason why *Perfect Fur You* wants to participate in the sponsorship program?

- ○ It is marvellous
- ○ Australian animals are endangered
- ● Modern development has badly affected animals
- ○ Australian animals are the cutest

If the question uses words from the text, always read the sentences that come before and after those words.

Why was the author interested in the ad?

- ○ It was in the newspaper last week
- ● The author's business wants to help animal conservation
- ○ The author was sad
- ○ The author thinks she is marvellous

For as long as I can remember, I've loved drawing funny little characters and making up stories about them. When I was five, I created a whole town of thumb print characters and pages of comic strip adventures about them.

I was forever trying to squeeze in time to watch one more cartoon before I went to school each morning. I'd save up my pocket money so I could see any new animated movie before it came out. This helped me understand what makes a good animated story.

As I got older, I became interested in computers and began creating short animations on my computer. I'd scan in my drawings, and then add colour and sound. Through these little 2–5 minute animations, I learnt the basics of computer animation and how to use the software I needed.

Try this

What helped the author understand what makes a good animated story?

- ◯ Being late to school in the morning
- ◯ Seeing cartoons at the movies and on TV
- ◯ Creating thumb print characters
- ◯ Saving up her pocket money

How did the author learn the basics of computer animation?

- ◯ She made short animations by scanning in her drawings
- ◯ She copied ideas from television cartoons
- ◯ She got older so it was easy
- ◯ It was easy once she added the colour and sound

MAKING INFERENCES

When you read or view a text, you often make assumptions or draw a conclusion from the information presented. In NAPLAN, you will be asked to answer inferential questions about events, settings and characters as well as illustrations or diagrams.

The answer to an inferential question will NOT be DIRECTLY stated in the text or pictures. You will need to look for reasons WHY something is the way it is.

Once upon a time deep in the forest lived three little wolves with their mother.

Every day, the wolves' mother would go out searching for food, while the little wolves played.

One day, however, the little wolves' mother did not return. They waited and waited but still she did not come back.

The next morning there was a loud knock on the front door. The eldest wolf tried to peek under the door.

"Wh…wh…who is it?" he enquired timidly.

"Why it is I, your friendly sales-pig. Can I come in?"

Why does the eldest wolf speak timidly?

- ○ He is a wolf so he can't talk properly
- ● He was afraid
- ○ He was speaking with a mouth full of food
- ○ He was holding his breath

You can infer that the wolf is afraid because he is stuttering "Wh...wh... who is it?"

Why does the sales-pig describe himself as 'friendly'?

- ○ He has lots of friends on Facebook
- ○ He smiles a lot
- ● He wants the wolves to think it is OK to talk to him
- ○ Everyone knows pigs are friendlier than wolves

To get the answer correct, you have to bring in your knowledge of the real fairy tale, The Three Little Pigs. Often the villain will pretend to be nice.

The Teacher

The teacher's coming round again,
Just like an endless train,
Huff and puff, and puff and huff
Testing out my brain.

I've never found it easy,
For thinking's quite a strain,
My mind is like a holey bucket,
Letting out the rain.

Try this

Why does the author say 'letting out the rain'?

- ◯ Her bucket has a hole in it
- ◯ The teacher left the windows open
- ◯ She is learning about the water cycle
- ◯ She can't remember anything

LITTLE BORING DAY SPA

Tired?? Worn out??
Hate early mornings??

Don't let Monday morning drag you down.

Why not leave the books, the tests, and the maths groups behind you and come and sample Little Boring's most relaxing day spa.

Upon arrival you will receive:

- a scalp massage
- light refreshments
- internationally renowned music therapy

Group discounts available, so bring your friends!

SHOP 1 NOSTRESS STREET, LITTLE BORING
PHONE: 5317707

Try this

Who is the target audience for this advertisement?

- ◯ School students
- ◯ People who get up late
- ◯ People who are bored
- ◯ People who have lots of friends

Do you give money to people who dress up as a cute, friendly marsupial? Well, if you do, you are not as smart as you look.

Many people say that any money spent on conservation is beneficial. That has proven not to be the case.
The $1.1 million spent on building a new enclosure for numbats, cannot possibly be as valuable as spending the same amount on regenerating natural habitat to save a whole colony of numbats in the wild. Any money spent should impact the entire species, not just a lucky few.

So when you put your gold coin in some group's collection jar, think about where it's going and what it's doing. There is a better way, and that is to work to protect our native landscapes, not our manufactured ones. Say no to animal sponsorship. Say yes to environmental protection.

Who is the audience for this text?

- ◯ People who like numbats
- ◯ People who dress up in animal costumes
- ◯ People who donate to animal welfare groups
- ◯ People who collect money to build zoo enclosures

Try this

If an author says 'you' they are talking to the reader. If they use 'we' they are joining themselves with the reader. If they use 'I' they are referring to themselves. If an author uses 'they', then the author is putting some distance between themselves, the characters and the audience.

Fighting the Good Fight

Emmeline Pankhurst fought as bravely as any other soldier to win her war!

Some trailblazers sail into the unknown in search of wealth and glory. Others, like Emmeline Pankhurst, come from the most unlikely backgrounds.

Emmeline was born in Manchester, England, in 1858. It was a time when women were supposed to have only one role – looking after the home. When she was twenty, Emmeline married Richard Pankhurst. Richard was a lawyer who chose to help the poor. When he died in 1898, Emmeline was left with four children to support.

Emmeline had seen her husband exhaust himself with many causes. So she thought it would be best to throw all her energies in one direction. In 1903, she formed the Women's Social and Political Union to campaign for women's suffrage – the right to vote.

From the article, what can you say about Emmeline Pankhurst?

- ◯ Not much, I don't know her
- ◯ She was a strong, determined woman
- ◯ She must be very old now
- ◯ She was exhausted

The author views Emmeline Pankhurst with ________________.

- ◯ admiration
- ◯ fear
- ◯ a telescope
- ◯ amusement

APPLIED COMPREHENSION

These are similar types of questions to making inferences. The answers to applied comprehension questions are not going to be directly stated in the text.

You may need to:

- combine information from the text and an illustration or diagram
- interpret or evaluate (make a judgement about) information or details
- identify the role and the position (point of view) of a narrator, character or author
- identify the motivation of a character for their actions
- identify the tone of a text (amusing, embarrassed, stubborn).

The Happy Wanderer

No strings to tie him down
The world is his to roam
The happy wanderer calls his pack
Any warm dry place will be his home

Frolicking, rollicking down the road
With a carefree attitude
The happy wanderer invites his friends
To join his playful mood.

One by one they join the parade
Padding feet and whipping tails
Bounding and boisterous is the chorus
Scattering leaves like wintry gales

"Padding feet and whipping tails"

Why is the wanderer's attitude 'carefree'?

- ● He can go wherever he likes
- ○ He has invited his friends to a party
- ○ It is winter time
- ○ He likes being noisy

Look at the first two lines of the poem.

Who is most likely to be the happy wanderer?

- ○ A horse
- ● A dog
- ○ A cowboy
- ○ A teacher

Why does the author use so many verbs in the poem?

- ○ She is bored
- ○ She is a fitness fanatic
- ○ She joined the parade
- ● She wanted to show how cheerful the wanderer is

Fishing Champion

John Medlow won the annual fishing competition at Noal Bay yesterday with a jewfish weighing 14 kilograms.

The fish put up quite a fight but John, with an enormous grin on his face, easily managed to reel it in.

"I couldn't believe my eyes!" John was heard to say to a bystander.

All the spectators admired the impressive catch. They were kept amused by a pelican trying to reach the fish as it was being weighed.

Look at the pronoun used in the text: his

Who is telling the story?

- ◯ A narrator
- ◯ The pelican
- ◯ John Medlow
- ◯ A bystander

Try this

Talaga Warna

On the day of the Princess's birthday, people from near and far gathered at the palace. They cheered when the King and Queen appeared with their daughter. His Majesty Prabu carefully handed the Princess a small, silken pillow. On it was draped the wonderful, jewelled necklace.

As he placed it gently around her graceful neck, the King said, "My beloved daughter, on this your 18th birthday, I present this gift to you from your parents and your people."

When the Princess looked down at the necklace, her eyes narrowed and her smile became thin and sharp.

"This is a piece of junk! It's ugly! I won't accept it!" she shouted so that all could hear.

She tore the necklace from her neck and threw it to the ground. The beautiful necklace lay broken at her feet, the precious gems scattered across the floor.

Which word best describes the Princess's reaction?

- ◯ Pleasant
- ◯ Regal
- ◯ Beloved
- ◯ Ungrateful

Be careful. Just because some of the answers are words from the text, they may not be the right answer.

The Money Tree

Our family had been under a bit of a financial strain lately, and my husband and I had told our children; Jenny 12, Rupert 8 and Louis 4, about how careful we needed to be because Dad had been retrenched and we no longer had the same amount of income.

My husband warned them that we didn't have a money tree in our backyard.

Later that afternoon, I went out the back to bring in the washing, when I saw Louis up to his elbows in dirt, digging a huge hole in the garden. I walked up and looked over his shoulder into the hole. He had put a $5 note at the bottom.

When I enquired as to why he was burying money in the dirt, he quite proudly told me that he was planting a money tree for Dad. He then asked, very seriously, if I knew how long they would take to grow.

If only!

Why does the text end with the words "If only!"?

Try this

- ◯ The author is not good at gardening
- ◯ The author wishes that money really did grow on trees
- ◯ Louis wishes he had more than a $5 note
- ◯ The author wants to be retrenched too

Marnie was deep in thought when she sensed someone close by. She swung her legs around so that they dangled off the edge of the bed and brushed against the carpet. Her father stood in the doorway, his gaunt face ashen with grief. Without saying a word, he entered the room, arms outstretched, and he embraced Marnie fiercely.

Marnie's heart skipped a beat. She thought she had prepared herself. But she had been dreadfully mistaken.

"She's been found," her father wept. "She's alive – but critical. They've taken her by helicopter to the intensive care unit."

As her father continued to cling to her, Marnie felt strangely detached from the whole situation. All she could say was "Oh." Over the years, Marnie had heard stories of families who faced the horror of not knowing the fate of a loved one, but the impact was far worse than she had ever imagined.

What would be a suitable title for this text?

Try this

____

VISUAL LITERACY

How to make a mummy

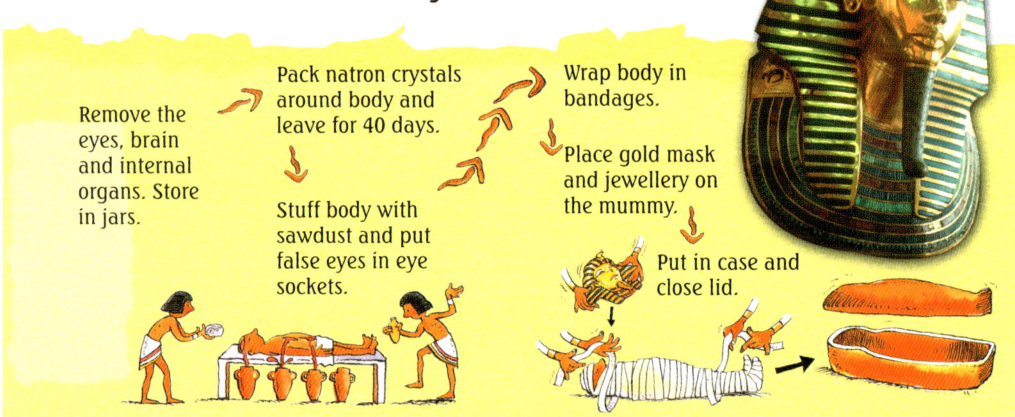

Think about the purpose of the text. It is a procedure so it will give instructions on HOW to do something.

What do the illustrations show?

- (●) The main steps in the process
- ( ) How many jars you need for the blood
- ( ) That it is good we don't make mummies now
- ( ) How difficult it is to mummify a body

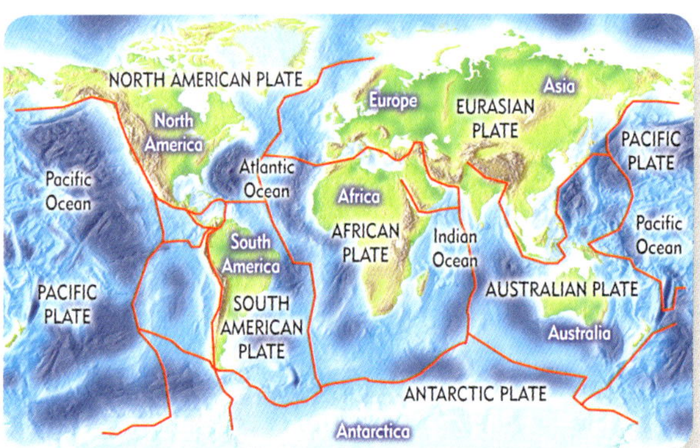

Go Fact – Earthquakes

San Francisco, in the USA, lies on the San Andreas Fault, which is at the edge of the North American and Pacific plates. When these plates slide against each other, earthquakes can occur. The 1906 earthquake was the most devastating earthquake in US history, killing approximately 3000 people.

Look for any captions or labels with the diagram. They can give you extra information.

Which statement is true?

- ( ) Tectonic plates have red edges
- ( ) Earthquakes only occur on the San Andreas Fault
- ( ) You must eat everything on your plate if you want dessert
- (●) Australia doesn't get many earthquakes because we are not close to the edge of a plate

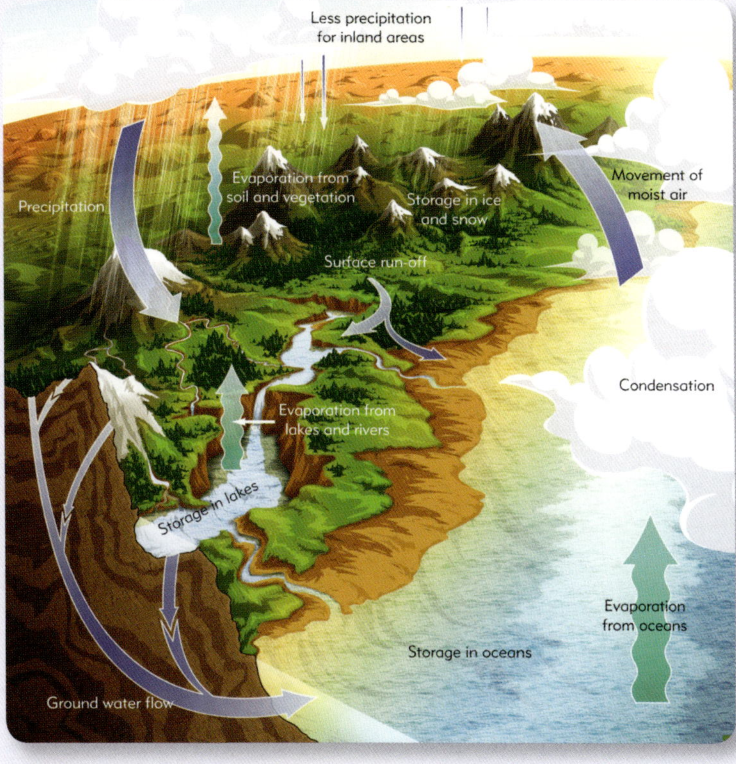

Which statement best suits the text?

- ◯ Precipitation comes from snowy mountains
- ◯ Inland areas get the most rain
- ◯ Melting snow increases surface run off
- ◯ Dry air is required for precipitation

Try this

1 The giraffe starts to munch on the spiky tree.

2 The tree takes quick action, pushing poison into its leaves.

3 Within 30 minutes the leaves are too poisonous to eat.

4 This tree sends a message to other trees. They then become poisonous as well. The giraffe moves on.

As its leaves fill with poison, they also release a gas. This signals other nearby acacia trees and they become poisonous as well.

From the text, we can conclude that:

- ◯ giraffes are dumb animals
- ◯ trees use telephones
- ◯ you should not eat spiky food
- ◯ giraffes will not feed at the same tree for a long time

Which of the following statements is NOT true?

- ◯ Only the leaves are always poisonous
- ◯ The acacia trees can sense gases in the air
- ◯ Giraffes like to eat acacia leaves
- ◯ After half an hour, a giraffe must move to another tree

SEQUENCING

When you are answering a sequencing question in NAPLAN, look out for words of phrases that signal time. For example: first, then, next, before that, a while later, in the meantime. These will help you to identify the events and put them in the correct order. Sometimes the question might relate to a diagram or illustration and not just the text, so use everything on the page to help give you the information you need.

Read through the text and underline the time-based words. Be careful to read the whole sentence because not all words have only one meaning.

In this example, the word 'next' relates to position rather than timing, so it is not an event used in the sequence.

Come to my house

"Hi Zoe! It's Sarah. I've checked with mum and she said that you can come over for afternoon tea. We've just made a chocolate cake with lots of sprinkles on top. Do you want to come?"

"Sure! I'd love too."

"Great! I'll tell you how to get here. Turn left after you walk out your front gate and go down Webb Street until you come to the big house. You know the one with the red roses that hang over the front fence. Next to this house is a narrow lane shaded by oak trees. Walk quickly down the lane because sometimes there is a hairy, black dog that lurks around looking for stray cats to chase. When you come to the end of the lane, turn right into Flint Street. You should be right next to the pharmacy. You can check out the fluffy toys in the window.

"Mum'll flip if I get any more!"

"I know! Anyway, then cross the road and continue along to the left. Before you get to the wooden bridge, hang a sharp right and…"

"Gee – how much further?"

"You're here! Look for the house with the red letter box out the front. That's me!"

"No worries. I'm leaving now! Don't eat all the cupcakes before I get there!"

Sequence the following:

- 3 Look for the red roses
- 1 Walk out the front gate
- 4 Avoid the scary dog
- 2 Turn left

Not all the answers have to use the same words as the text. Look for similar meanings.

Try this

The life cycle of a star

The length of a star's life depends on how much material it contains.

Within a nebula, gas and dust particles are drawn together by gravity. The particles begin spinning to form a disc. This is called a protostar.

As the protostar shrinks, the particles rub together and begin to warm up. A halo of gas and dust forms around the core.

When the temperature reaches 15 million degrees Celsius, nuclear fusion begins in the core, and hydrogen is converted into helium. The halo of gas and dust is blown away by the released energy.

Energy explodes outwards in the form of heat and light. The star shines into space. During this period of its life, the star is known as a main sequence star.

Sequence the following statements.

- ☐ Dust particles create heat through friction
- ☐ The particles within a nebula begin to rotate
- ☐ Energy radiates out from the star
- ☐ Helium is created

How is electricity generated?

Try this

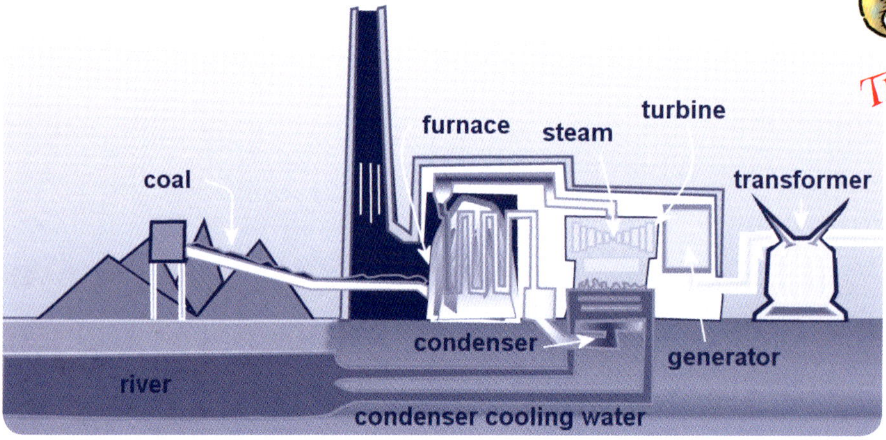

First, the power station burns the coal at extremely high temperatures. This causes the water to turn into steam.

→

The steam is then forced, at very high pressure, into a turbine (a series of fans with a central shaft). When the steam pushes against these fans, they turn. Because the fans are attached to the central shaft, it turns as well.

→

This spinning shaft is linked to a generator.
The generator has a central magnet (a rotor) inside a number of electrical coils. When the turbine turns the shaft, the coils rotate between the magnets. This magnetic field passing over the coils causes electricity to follow in the wire.

↓

The electricity moves through the wire to a step-up transformer when it is boosted to a high voltage so that it can travel over long distances.

←

The high voltage electricity then travels through huge cables held up on pylons. When it is closer to where it is needed, the electricity passes through a step-down transformer to reduce its voltage again.

←

At last the electricity reaches the consumer. What would your day be like without it?

What wouldn't you need if the electricity didn't have to travel very far?

- ◯ A transformer
- ◯ A rotor
- ◯ A magnetic field
- ◯ A turbine

Explain why you think the steam has to be pumped into the turbine at very high pressure.

____

____

____

THE MAIN IDEA

Read the text and answer the questions below.

Racing in the streets

You're speeding down a road, flat on your back on a special skateboard. You've got no brakes and you're only a few centimetres above the ground. That's street luge. It is based on a winter sport where people hurtle down winding frozen tubes at amazing speeds.

Anyone who's ridden a bicycle or a skateboard too fast knows about hitting the ground. At 110 kilometres per hour, the gravel rash can be deadly. Lugers have to wear full-face helmets and clothing that is streamlined but very strong.

What is the main idea of this text?

- ● Street luge is fast but dangerous
- ○ Gravel rash hurts
- ○ Street luge is a sport for lazy people
- ○ Only people who ride bikes and skateboards can do street lugestorm

The main idea is what the text is MOSTLY about. It is often found at the beginning or at the end of a text.

The middle part of the text contains the facts and details that match the main idea.

Try this

Science on the case

The best way to catch criminals is to catch them 'red handed' in the act of committing the crime. Of course, in most cases that is not what happens. Instead, teams of forensic scientists use science to solve crimes. They can often point the finger at a suspect – and prove that he or she did it!

At the scene of a crime, police detectives take detailed notes and photographs, interview witnesses and look for clues. They also organise the team of forensic scientists. But the forensic scientists don't just look for evidence that will support the detective's theory. It is their job to uncover the facts, even if it proves a suspect didn't do it.

Each member of the forensic team has his or her own job.

Crime Scene Investigators (or CSIs) examine the scene and collect evidence.

Lab-based scientists carefully analyse all this material, often using the latest technology.

Medical forensic scientists, such as pathologists and dentists, are called in if they are needed.

What is the main idea of this text?

____

REASONING

These types of questions ask you to assess or evaluate information in order to make a judgement as to WHY something happened, or they may ask you to choose an idea, moral or message that best matches the text.

The answer won't be given directly in the text, so you will need to look for clues, words with similar meanings and conjunctions that link ideas between sentences and paragraphs.

A Strange and Deadly Triangle

During the past three centuries, an estimated 2000 vessels and 75 aircraft have mysteriously vanished over the Bermuda triangle (that part of the Atlantic Ocean between Miami Florida in the USA, the island of Bermuda and the island of Puerto Rico).

The most famous of these disappearances was that of Flight 19 in 1945. An entire squadron of Avenger torpedo bombers (five in total) vanished. The planes took off from Florida on the coast of America for a practice bombing run. The transmission from the flight indicated that the compasses weren't working properly. As the planes continued to fly, radio transmissions became increasingly more difficult. Eventually contact was lost and all the planes just disappeared. Incredibly, another plane with a thirteen man crew was sent out to search for the missing planes and it never returned.

Why does the last sentence start with the word 'incredibly'?

- ◯ Who would want to fly out into a dangerous area?
- ● It is unusual that so many planes would be lost
- ◯ Not many planes carry thirteen men
- ◯ Florida is so nice that no one wants to leave it

Read the last sentence where the word 'incredibly' comes from. The final words say "... and it too never returned."

Which word best describes the Bermuda Triangle?

- ◯ sunny
- ◯ equilateral
- ● puzzling
- ◯ coastal

You need to look for words in the text that describe the Bermuda Triangle and what happened there such as "mysteriously". The correct answer uses a synonym of mysterious.

Try this

Would You Buy It?

On 1st April 1998, a company in America advertised a left-handed hamburger for left-handed burger eaters. The new hamburger was supposed to be heavier on the left so the fillings wouldn't spill out on the right. Thousands of customers tried to order the left-handed burgers.

Would you like to lose weight through your feet?
On 1 April 2000, an English newspaper claimed you could – with Fatsox. Just sweat the fat into the socks and then wash the fat away.
Was this for real?
Fat chance!

Which idea best matches the text?

- ◯ It is best to lose weight through your feet
- ◯ Left-handed burger customers are messy eaters
- ◯ Lots of left-handed people eat burgers
- ◯ Don't believe everything you see in advertising

Try this

Should gorillas be removed from their natural habitats?

There are three subspecies of gorillas living in Africa – the western lowland gorilla, the eastern lowland gorilla and the mountain gorilla – and all are endangered. Mountain gorillas are particularly at risk, because there are only about 620 living, with none in captivity. Most zoos conducting gorilla breeding programs are using the gorillas they already hold in captivity, and have agreed not to take gorillas from the wild. Is zoo breeding the only way to ensure the survival of gorillas?

Gorillas have a slow rate of reproduction. But in 1995, a cooperative project between two zoos using in-vitro fertilisation and embryo transfer resulted in a lowland baby gorilla. If more gorillas were kept in zoos, they could use and improve upon these techniques to increase the rate of reproduction.

The lifespan of gorillas in the wild is 30 to 40 years, where they face the constant threat of habitat destruction and illegal poaching. Whereas in zoos, their life span can be up to 50 years, and with primate research intensifying, this could increase even further.

Even though zoos cannot hope to completely reproduce the natural environment of each gorilla species, due to the imminent risk of extinction, it is vital that many are kept in zoos in the hope of using artificial techniques to keep the species away from the brink.

In the third paragraph, the text says 'this could increase even further', what does this mean?

- ◯ Gorillas could get even bigger
- ◯ Gorillas could live longer
- ◯ Gorillas could have more babies
- ◯ The risk of extinction will increase

FIGURATIVE LANGUAGE

Figurative language is used most often in descriptive or narrative type texts. It is where you compare two things, or use words which have a different meaning to what you might expect. There are many different types of figurative language. They include:

Onomatopoeia The sound of a word is mirrored in its meaning. E.g. screech, woosh, clunk, bang	**Simile** The comparison of two things using 'like' or 'as'. E.g. The principal's face was as red as a beetroot when he was yelling at the students. She ran like the wind as she was chased by the dog.
Metaphor The comparison of two things, saying one IS the other. E.g. the howling wolf battered against the windows (the howling wolf is the wind)	**Personification** This is where inanimate objects are given human characteristics. E.g. the coffee grinder ate its meal and then spat it out into the cup.
Alliteration A repeated consonant sound. E.g. Goofy Gavin grabbed a green grape.	**Assonance** A repeated vowel sound. E.g. Oh no! Off to work we go in the deep white snow.
Idiom A word, phrase or saying that cannot be taken literally. The combination of the words has a different meaning to the meaning of the individual words. E.g. I was in the doghouse because I didn't do my homework. (I was in trouble because I didn't do my homework.)	

Saving Atlantis

So far, Flynn had spent as little time as possible at the site. He preferred to spend his days listening to the old Greek fishermen, in the cafes that lined the harbour.

Today, two men had entertained him with a story about a scary woman called Medusa. She was once very beautiful but had been changed into an old hag with serpents for hair. "Talk about a bad hair day!" laughed Flynn when the men described her. She was so monstrous that her stare would turn people to stone. Flynn shivered at the thought of meeting her. Like all the other stories he had been told, this one had him glued to his seat. It was after he left the old men and their story, however, that Flynn's day became really interesting.

This is an idiom. So think about what Flynn means when he says he was 'glued to his seat' not the actual meaning of being glued to a seat.

If Flynn was 'glued to his seat', he...

○ had a sticky bottom
● didn't want to leave
○ was laughed at by the old men
○ was embarrassed

Try this

The text suggests that the fire is:

○ alive
○ slow moving
○ being extinguished
○ harmless

In the second verse, when the fire went 'through the brakes' it sounded like:

○ angry snakes
○ distant gun shots
○ the wind
○ a sweeping broom

A Fire at Ross' Farm, by Banjo Paterson

One Christmas time, when months of drought
Had parched the western creeks,
The bush-fires started in the north
And travelled south for weeks.
At night along the river-side
The scene was grand and strange–
The hill-fires looked like lighted streets
Of cities in the range.

The cattle-tracks between the trees
Were like long dusky aisles,
And on a sudden breeze the fire
Would sweep along for miles;
Like sounds of distant musketry
It crackled through the brakes,
And o'er the flat of silver grass
It hissed like angry snakes.

It leapt across the flowing streams
And raced o'er pastures broad;
It climbed the trees and lit the boughs
And through the scrubs it roared.

The Lion and the Mouse

One warm summer's day, deep in the savannah, a tiny field mouse was scurrying here and there, trying to gather food for his family.

The mouse was blinded by his important task and didn't see the paw of a gigantic lion, poking out from behind the tall grass. He scurried right over the top of it.

"Thwaack!"

"How dare you wake me from my midday nap," roared the lion, picking up the terrified mouse by its tail. "I think I will just gobble you up to teach you a lesson."

As the mouse was slowly lowered into the dark, wet cave, he managed to squeak, "Oh please don't kind King. I beg of you, release me. Who will care for my two thousand, three hundred and forty-one children if I am gone?"

"So many? Are you mad?" gasped the lion incredulously. "I can hardly have that many mice running around the savannah looking to take revenge on me for devouring their father. Alright, you are free to go. But take care, next time I may not be so forgiving."

"Oh thank you! I will always remember your kindness."

So the mouse scurried off back to his family, and the lion went back to his nap, forgetting the whole incident.

Several weeks later, whilst roaming the savannah, the lion was caught in a hunter's trap. The more he struggled, the more ensnared he became. He had almost given up when he heard tiny typewriters in his head.

"We meet again kind King," said a voice.

"What? Who? Why?" queried the lion.

"It is I, the mouse you didn't eat. I saw your struggles and I have called my children to come and help. Soon you will be free." The little mouse and his three thousand, one hundred and fifteen children gnawed away at the strong thick ropes until finally the lion was released. After all, one good turn deserves another.

Why was the mouse blind?

- ◯ He was concentrating on his work
- ◯ He couldn't see
- ◯ He was confused
- ◯ He was hungry

What were the typewriters?

- ◯ The author typing this story
- ◯ The lion's teeth chattering because he was scared
- ◯ The sound of the mice's teeth chewing at the rope
- ◯ The sound of the mice's teeth because it was cold

PUNCTUATION AND ITS PURPOSE

In the NAPLAN reading test, you may be asked some questions that involve punctuation and how its use affects the reading of the text and what its purpose is in the text.

For more information on different types of punctuation and how or when they are used go to pages 114–116 in the writing section.

A secret letter scramble

Julius Caesar was a very famous and successful Roman general in ancient times. His armies usually won their battles because Caesar was good at planning what his troops should do next. When Caesar sent a message to tell his troops what to do, he didn't want his enemies to be able to read it. So Caesar invented his own secret code – the Caesar cipher.

Why has the author used a dash in the last sentence?

- ○ She was lazy
- ○ There is a word missing
- ○ The pen slipped
- ● To emphasise the name of the code

Try this

Trapdoor Spiders

Spiders are arachnids and are members of the arthropod group of invertebrates. The trapdoor spider, also known as the burrowing spider, secures its burrow by spinning a hinged door of silk over the opening.

Trapdoor spiders live mainly in tropical regions and are common in the south and west of the United States. They prefer steep slopes and sandy soil.

These spiders are terrestrial. They dig their burrow by lifting the soil with their jaws. Then they use their hind legs to remove the soil. The spiders then line their burrow with silk. Finally, they use ground debris to camouflage the burrow from the prying eyes of predators.

What is the purpose of the commas used in the first paragraph?

- ○ They have no purpose
- ○ To contain additional information
- ○ They are used instead of a full stop
- ○ They are used to separate fact from fiction

PRACTICE READING TEST

Over the next few pages, there are several sample texts and questions to help you prepare for NAPLAN. There are a range of different types of texts and questions. If you get stuck, check out some of the previous activities and tips to help you.

How blood moves around your body

Your heart is a large muscle which is found in the centre of your chest. It works like a very strong pump – moving the blood around your body.

Each person's heart is divided into four chambers – two ventricles and two atria. You feel the contraction of these chambers as a heartbeat. The heart contracts, or squeezes itself, about once every second. This contraction sends blood flowing throughout the body.

First, your blood moves from the left atrium to the left ventricle, and then is carried away from your heart by a large artery called the aorta. The aorta leads to smaller arteries, which are the vessels that carry blood away from your heart. The arteries flow into very small vessels called capillaries.

Next, the capillaries join with thin-walled veins (blood vessels that carry blood towards your heart). These smaller veins connect with bigger veins, which flow into the large vein called the vena cava. It is the vena cava which enters the right atrium of your heart.

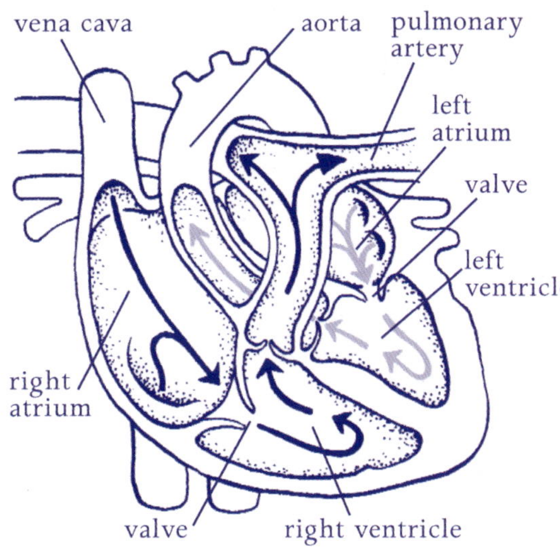

After your blood has moved from the right atrium to the right ventricle, it goes to the lungs to be oxygenated. Finally the blood returns to the heart, via the left atrium and the circulation of blood continues.

For further details, please contact your doctor or The National Heart Foundation.

The Quest for the Cup

Heavy thumps and loud crashes filled the darkness. The strange noises jolted Flynn awake. Mia was already up looking for her favourite companion. "Got it," she whispered turning on the flashlight. She stood just like a general, head to one side, listening intently to what was going on downstairs.

"Burglars!" hissed Mia. "Come on Flynn, it sounds like they're in Uncle Earl's study." As they crept down the stairway, Mia grabbed a carved spear (one of her Uncle's mementoes) off the wall.

"We're being ro....robbed?" stammered Flynn, helping himself to an ancient Chinese sword.

They stood either side of the study door, listening to the heavy footsteps coming from within. A faint strip of light shone at the bottom of the door.

"They're ripping the place apart!" whispered Flynn, turning to go back upstairs.

"Hey," urged Mia. "Uncle Earl's life work is in that study. On the count of three I'm going in... Ready?"

Flynn wiped his sweaty palms on his pyjamas, gripped his sword and nodded.

Mia mouthed, "One...two...three!" and Flynn threw the door wide open. He leapt inside with a bloodcurdling scream.

"Drop it now!" demanded Mia.

Uncle Earl was standing at the top of a ladder leaning against a bookshelf. As he turned, startled, he dropped a small box. There was a loud crash as it landed on the floor. Uncle Earl raised his arms in surrender. Mia and Flynn stared at the floor of the study. It was a gigantic mess of books, papers, folders, videos, CDs and overflowing boxes.

"Uncle Earl?" cried Mia. "What are you doing?"

Concert Review

The Butcher's Butcher it!

By: Ima Notlikenit

I'm struggling to think of a more useless waste of time than listening to The Butchers crank out their mindless neo punk. Man they were BAD. The Butchers need a talent transplant. Guys, if you are going to play other people's songs, then at least play them in tune. Then again, why are you playing other people's songs? Can't you write your own?

Take the old porter classic, *Don't Fence Me In*. I saw it sung in a movie once. And now I've seen it destroyed on stage by The Butchers. The song was an angry mess of shouting and guitar distortion, and then they smashed the drum kit. Well done guys. You really rock.

The Butchers Speak Our Language

By: Hiya Imsonice

If you like your music with brains, make sure you catch The Butchers on tour this month. Your reviewer was privileged to see them perform last week, and I can't get the smile off my face.

The Butchers are great interpreters of classic songs. They take songs from an earlier age and rebuild them in well-crafted neo punk. In doing so, they explore the human experience – loneliness, anger, joy, laughter and tears. Having said that, I would like to see what they could come up with as an original piece. It would be a true test of artistry.

Concert Review (continued)

One excellent example of their interpretive skills was the old Porter classic *Don't Fence Me In*. On one level it's a simple tale about love of the land and wide open spaces. But The Butchers understand the song's subtext of isolation and cowboy stereotypes. Not to be "fenced in" can be lonely. When the drummer kicked over his drum kit, he was making a statement about his need as an artist not to be "fenced in". It was a powerful comment on the pressures of modern society. Well done guys. You've returned intelligence to music and made us think again.

Types of Waste

Homes and industries produce biodegradable, non-biodegradable and hazardous waste.

Decomposing naturally

Biodegradable waste is anything that decomposes naturally such as food scraps, egg shells and grass clippings. Micro-organisms break down the waste into water, carbon dioxide and minerals, which nourish plants and improve soil quality. Most organic materials, such as food scraps and paper are biodegradable. Some types of plastic made from plants are also biodegradable.

If biodegradable waste is buried in landfills with other types of waste, it will not have the oxygen, light and water it requires to decompose.

Here for a long time

Non-biodegradable waste will not break down naturally and must be recycled, burnt or buried.

A common non-biodegradable product is the plastic shopping bag. Plastic bags take anywhere between 15 and 1000 years to break down in the environment. Every year, they also kill at least 100 000 birds, whales, seals and turtles that choke on the bags or become trapped in them.

Shops and governments are trying to reduce the use of bags by either charging shoppers for each bag they use, or banning them altogether.

Handle carefully

Waste that burns or explodes, or is toxic to people or the environment, is known as hazardous waste. It is usually the by-product of industrial processes, but common household products used for cleaning and gardening are also hazardous when thrown away.

Like non-biodegradable waste, some hazardous wastes can be recycled. For example, engine oils can be cleaned and reused, or burnt to provide energy.

Shade one bubble

Read How blood moves around your body and answer questions 1 to 5

1. What is the purpose of the text?

- ◯ To keep your heart healthy
- ◯ To explain the circulatory system
- ◯ To describe the heart
- ◯ To make your heart beat faster

2. Why are brackets used in the fourth paragraph?

- ◯ To provide a definition
- ◯ To replace the need for another sentence
- ◯ To replace an illustration
- ◯ To describe what happens next

3. If the heart muscle is not contracting, then ___________

- ◯ you should stop reading the text
- ◯ your lungs need to work harder
- ◯ the blood needs less oxygen
- ◯ blood stops flowing

4. Write the numbers 2 to 5 in the boxes to show the order of events in the text.

- ☐ The blood leaves the right ventricle
- ☐ The blood leaves via the left ventricle
- 1 The blood travels through the vena cava
- ☐ Oxygenated blood returns to the heart
- ☐ The blood travels around your body

5. The information in this text is best described as ___________

- ◯ disgusting
- ◯ the digestive system
- ◯ a cycle
- ◯ opinionated

Read The Quest for the Cup and answer questions 6 to 10

6. Flynn can best be described as ______

- ◯ young and silly
- ◯ tired and bored
- ◯ frightened and reluctant
- ◯ brave and fearless

7. Mia's attitude towards Uncle Earl's life work is __________

- ◯ uninterested
- ◯ protective
- ◯ humorous
- ◯ frustrated

8. Mia's favourite companion is ______

- ◯ Flynn
- ◯ the burglar
- ◯ Uncle Earl
- ◯ her torch

Write your answer

9. How did Flynn feel before he and Mia entered the study? How do you know? Explain your answer.

____

____

____

____

____

10. Why does the author use an ellipsis before Mia says "Ready?" ?

- ◯ To show that she waits for Flynn
- ◯ The typist made a mistake
- ◯ It is because Mia counted to three
- ◯ Mia is stammering because she is frightened

Read Concert Review (both texts) and answer questions 11 to 14

11. What do both texts agree on?

- ◯ The Butchers cut meat
- ◯ The Butchers are fantastic musicians
- ◯ The Butchers should sing their own songs
- ◯ The Butchers don't like fences

12. Why does the author Ima Notlikenit use the term "Guys" in the first paragraph?

- ◯ She is addressing the reader directly
- ◯ She is talking directly to the band
- ◯ She is addressing the audience at the concert
- ◯ She wants to sound cool because she is reviewing a rock band

13. What do fences most strongly represent for the drummer?

- ◯ Lack of freedom
- ◯ Farm animals
- ◯ Bad music
- ◯ Intelligence

14. Which idea best matches these texts?

- ◯ Neo punk music is awful
- ◯ Butchers should stick to making sausages
- ◯ Music reviewers don't know what they are talking about
- ◯ Not everyone has the same opinions

Read Types of Waste and answer questions 15 to 19

15. To decompose, apple peels need ________________

- ◯ water, carbon dioxide and minerals
- ◯ to be dumped in landfill
- ◯ water, oxygen and light
- ◯ to be burnt

16. The text uses subheadings to:

- ◯ draw the reader's attention to different information
- ◯ take up more space on the page
- ◯ make the text look more important
- ◯ separate the pictures and diagrams

17. What does 'them' refer to in the section "Here for a long time"?

- ◯ Biodegradable waste products
- ◯ Plastic shopping bags
- ◯ Birds, whales, seals and turtles
- ◯ Recycled materials

18. Which statement best matches the text?

- ◯ We need more landfill sites for biodegradable waste
- ◯ Governments should ban all shopping bags
- ◯ Hazardous waste is recycled
- ◯ Different categories of waste have different treatment methods

19. According to the text, which of the following statements is NOT true?

- ◯ We use toxic materials in our homes
- ◯ If products cost more, we use them less
- ◯ Biodegradable waste must be recycled
- ◯ Micro-organisms help to decompose paper products

END OF TEST

WRITING

When you are in the test, the teachers cannot help you think of ideas or explain any of the pictures to you. They can only read the instructions which are on the stimulus page.

The NAPLAN writing test is different to the reading, language conventions and numeracy tests. There are no multiple choice questions or short answer questions. Instead you are provided with a single page of images and text as a stimulus and three lined pages to write on.

You will be asked to write a specific type of text:

1. Persuasive (such as an argument/exposition or discussion)
2. Imaginative (such as a narrative)
3. Informative (such as a procedure, report or explanation)

While the test takes 40 minutes to complete, you do not actually have 40 minutes of writing time.

The test is organised as:

Planning: 5 minutes

Writing: 30 minutes

Editing/Checking: 5 minutes

Use your planning time well. Create a flow chart of events, a list of arguments, supporting evidence, subheadings or key words to help you along the way.

Getting started

Do you sometimes find it tricky to think quickly on the spot and get started? Well don't worry. You will not have to jump straight in to writing as soon as the test starts.

To begin with, you will be given 5 minutes to plan your writing. In the past, schools and teachers have been informed of the type of text to be tested beforehand, so you should know in advance if you will be writing a narrative, persuasive or informative text.

PERSUASIVE TEXTS

Writing that is **persuasive** tries to get the audience to agree with a point of view. As an author of a persuasive text, you may:

- give your own opinion and use personal experiences
- use the opinions of other people (experts)
- discuss different sides of the issue
- evaluate the issue.

In a persuasive text, you must have a sense of authority about the topic so the reader believes you.

Types of persuasive texts

When writing your persuasive text for NAPLAN, you may choose to write:

a) an exposition (sometimes known as an argument)

Exposition texts are written for the purpose of presenting a point of view in favour or against a specific topic. The ultimate aim is to try to convince the reader to agree with your opinion, or take a certain course of action, by giving reasons and examples to support your ideas.

Exposition texts:

- are emotive
- are biased
- sound authoritative

Structure:

Introduction
- ✷ include a statement to give the author's opinion
- ✷ preview important arguments
- ✷ engage the reader's attention

Body
- ✷ include a series of paragraphs
- ✷ give a new idea or argument with reasons and examples to support it in each paragraph
- ✷ use persuasive language
- ✷ use quoted or reported speech
- ✷ use cohesive language to link ideas between paragraphs

Conclusion
- ✷ restate the position of the writer
- ✷ sum up the main arguments
- ✷ include request action to be taken by the reader (optional)
- ✷ does NOT give any new information

b) a discussion

Discussion texts are written for the purpose of presenting different opinions, points of view, or perspectives on a specific issue. These may be:

- in favour
- against
- unsure

Ideas and arguments from all sides are evaluated before a decision is made.

Discussion texts:

- can examine controversial topics
- need to be convincing
- use arguments directly related to the topic
- sound authoritative

Structure:

Introduction

* include a statement to define the topic
* give background information to the reader about the topic
* show the different points of view to be examined

Body

* include a series of paragraphs
* include 2 or 3 paragraphs with arguments in favour and reasons or examples to support these ideas
* include 2 or 3 paragraphs with arguments against and reasons or examples to support these ideas
* use quoted or reported speech
* use persuasive language
* use cohesive language to link ideas or to show change of opinion

Conclusion

* give a summary of arguments from both sides
* evaluate which arguments are the most effective
* recommend one point of view over the other because of the arguments presented

How will my persuasive writing be marked?

The teachers who mark all the NAPLAN writing tests use the same marking criteria so no matter who you are, what your school is, or where you live, you are marked in the same way as everyone else.

The marking criteria have 10 different sections. Each section is marked separately, so if you don't do well in one section, you can still do well in all the others.

Persuasive criteria summary

AUDIENCE (the people who will be reading the text)		**Scoring range 0–6**
Weaker texts	**Standard texts**	**Stronger texts**
* Are very short * Are very simple * Copy the stimulus material * Try to make the reader familiar with the topic	* Try to persuade * Allow the reader to identify the issue * Allow the reader to understand the information * Try to create a relationship with the author (friendly/informative/expert)	* Give solid and appropriate reasons for arguments * Are consistent with their information * Engage the audience well * Use values to make a point * Change or challenge the expectations of the reader

Example texts:	
Standard text	Most children love to get outside and run around. It is much better than being stuck in a boring classroom. So why not make them play a team sport? Sports such as soccer, netball and oztag involve lots of players at the same time, so no one will be left out. The best part about playing a team sport is that you can have fun with your friends and get fit and healthy at the same time. Would you want to be the only person left sitting on the sideline getting fat? Well then go on and join a team!
Stronger text	Sweaty socks. Filthy clothes. Bumps, bruises and broken bones. Is that the image you have when you think of kids sport? Or perhaps you like to watch and giggle at the six year old boys playing soccer as if they were seagulls fighting over a couple of chips! Well, despite the sometimes accident prone nature of children's sport, it can actually be quite good for them. Nowadays the media is filled with stories and case studies of childhood obesity. We all shake our heads and say 'how terrible'. But when parents are asked to let their sons play rugby it's a completely different story. "Oh no!" they shudder. "They can't play that. It's far too dangerous." Sure, the possibility of a broken arm isn't exactly appealing. But it is certainly better than heart disease, diabetes or stroke, as overweight kids become overweight adults and suffer chronic health problems. Don't you agree?

Coloured text is: Weaker level Standard level Stronger level

STRUCTURE (how the text is organised)		**Scoring range 0–4**
Weaker texts	**Standard texts**	**Stronger texts**
* Use the wrong text type * Have only one big section * Have just a list of statements * Do not use any evidence to prove a point	* Have at least two structural sections * May have an introduction, body and conclusion but they are not strong * The introduction makes a simple statement of position	* Have all three sections * The body has detailed reasons and evidence * All three sections are well developed * The introduction has a clear position * The conclusion reflects the issues and may recommend or demand some action

Example texts:

Standard text

Participating in friendly competition through playing team sports is an important part of being a kid.

Children develop their ability to work together and cooperate. They learn to think on their feet and make strategic decisions. Doctors have found that children who are physically active do better at schoolwork.

So often, we hear about children behaving badly because they are bored. Well, let them join a sporting team.

In conclusion, playing a team sport has many positive effects on children. They develop personal fitness, and learn to respect team mates and opponents.

Stronger text

Sweaty skin, smelly people and dirty socks is how many kids see sport. Relaxing in their lounge room, curled up with an ipod or PlayStation is their idea of fun. Yet many adults say that playing a team sport is a good idea. In fact, they nag their children to become more physically active. But why should they bother?

Participation in a team sport is a vital learning experience. Through team sports, children develop their ability to work together and cooperate. They also learn to think on their feet and make strategic decisions. Doctors have found that children who are physically active do better at schoolwork than children who spend most of their time watching TV.

So often, we hear about children behaving badly because they are bored. Well, let them join a sporting team. Last week, Dave Rikard from 'Sports for Kids' told parents, "Between training, playing the game and all the fun social activities involved, there isn't a lot of time left for boredom. Kids who play team sports learn about respect and responsibility, as well as the importance of a healthy lifestyle."

As you can see, playing a team sport has many positive effects on children. From developing personal fitness to learning to respect team mates and opponents, children who play sport are better off than those who don't. So stop lying around on the couch complaining about being bored, join a team and get involved today!

Coloured text is: Weaker level   Standard level   Stronger level

IDEAS

Scoring range 0–5

(what you say in the text – your arguments, reasons or evidence to support them)

Weaker texts	Standard texts	Stronger texts
* The ideas are not related to the topic OR * Have only one idea OR * There are a few simple ideas related to the topic, but they have only very basic details	* At least one idea is well developed with good detail * There are a few ideas but not all of them are very persuasive * Most of the ideas are personal and/or family based	* Include most ideas that have relevant detail * The ideas look at more than just personal ideas * Have ideas that use wider world issues * Include ideas that are very persuasive * Include ideas that explain cause and effect and argue against the opinions of others

Example texts:

Standard text

Washing, ironing, vacuuming, doing the dishes. Should children have to do such boring, dirty jobs? Definitely not!

To begin with, in this age of modern technology, most household jobs require the use of electric appliances. It is far too dangerous to allow young children access to boiling hot water, electrical cords and power points. Parents are supposed to look after their children, not put them in harm's way.

Now adults may argue that children should do jobs around the house. They mistakenly believe that it develops a sense of responsibility. What rubbish!

Work is for adults and play is for children. It is as simple as that!

Stronger text

Washing, ironing, vacuuming, doing the dishes. Should children have to do such boring, dirty jobs? Definitely not!

To begin with, in this age of modern technology, most household jobs require the use of electric appliances. It is far too dangerous to allow young children access to boiling hot water, electrical cords and power points. Parents are supposed to look after their children, not put them in harm's way.

Now adults may argue that children should do jobs around the house. They mistakenly believe that it develops a sense of responsibility. What rubbish! All it does it make children resentful and cranky and create family arguments. How is that helpful?

As usual, those people who expect children to work like slaves are only looking at it from the point of view of the adults. But what about the children? Our tender young minds need care and nurturing, not soap and brooms. Everyone shakes their head and says 'how terrible Cinderella's step mother was to make her do all the household chores', yet that is what some people are arguing for today. Is this right? Of course not!

Work is for adults and play is for children. It is as simple as that!

Coloured text is: Weaker level Standard level Stronger level

PERSUASIVE DEVICES (the ways you try and persuade the reader) Scoring range 0–4

Weaker texts	Standard texts	Stronger texts
* Use simple persuasive devices such as think, should, very, because * State personal opinion	* Use some persuasive devices to support the writer's opinion such as 'for example' * Appeal directly to the audience using pronoun 'you' * Use 'expert' opinions to gain reader respect for the ideas mentioned	* Effectively use different persuasive devices * Appeal to values and emotions * Argue against the views of others

Check out page 58 for more information about persuasive devices.

If your text is short (less than 1 page), even if you use persuasive devices well, you may not score top marks.

Example texts:

Standard text

Household chores. Whether you like them or hate them, they still have to be done.

Our lives today are really busy. Everyone is rushing around with work, sport and social activities. That means that everyone in a family should help out at home. There are plenty of jobs that even the youngest child can do. It might be as simple as folding the washing or sweeping the kitchen floor. It really isn't hard.

Now clearly most children would rather not do jobs around the house. They would much prefer to be outside playing. But if only kids understood that by helping around the house, mum and dad would be able to spend more time being with them and sharing new experiences with them.

I see no good reason why children should not help out at home. After all, families are supposed to stick together.

Stronger text

Household chores. Whether you like them or hate them, they still have to be done. But who should do them?

Our lives today are really busy. Everyone is rushing around with work, sport and social activities. Surely that means that everyone in a family should help out at home? There are plenty of jobs that even the youngest child can do. It might be as simple as folding the washing or sweeping the kitchen floor. It really isn't hard is it?

Now clearly most children would rather not do jobs around the house. They would much prefer to be outside playing. Who wouldn't? But if only kids understood that by helping around the house, mum and dad would be able to spend more time being with them and sharing new experiences with them. One local mother who was asked about this said, "I spend so long cleaning up after the kids that I am so exhausted I don't even have the energy to take them to the park after school."

I see no good reason why children should not help out at home. After all, families are supposed to stick together aren't they?

Coloured text is: Weaker level Standard level Stronger level

VOCABULARY (the types of words used)		Scoring range 0–5
Weaker texts	**Standard texts**	**Stronger texts**
* Have very short text * Use mostly simple content words * May have 2–3 precise words or phrases * Rely on words modelled in the stimulus material	* Sometimes use simple words – think, need, very, always. * Use some (around 4–6) precise words or phrases – urge, solution, protect, rarely, it is highly unlikely	* Consistently use many different precise words * Include writing that is fluent and articulate

Example texts:

Standard text	Delicious soups, fresh breads and sweet desserts. These are just some of the wonderful foods you could create if you learnt how to cook. Learning to create tasty meals for friends and family is also a part of our way of life. When we gather for weddings, birthdays or other special occasions, how do we celebrate? Well with food of course! So next time someone in your family suggests you go out to grab a greasy hamburger for dinner, stop them and say, "How about we make our own?" It is sure to be tastier, healthier and lots more fun.
Stronger text	Exotic spicy soups, warm crusty breads and best of all, tantalising desserts. These are just some of the culinary delights you could create if you learnt how to cook. But should you bother? Without a doubt, cooking is a skill that everyone in our community should master. After all, food is one of the essentials for life. Without it we die! Although poor dietary decision making and poor food hygiene also lead to many deaths each year from obesity and food poisoning. This is why the education that comes from learning how to cook properly is vital. Learning to create tasty meals for friends and family is also a crucial part of our way of life. When we gather for weddings, birthdays or other special occasions, how do we celebrate? Well with food of course! So next time someone in your family recommends that you go out to grab a greasy hamburger for dinner, stop them and say, "How about we make our own?" It is sure to be tastier, healthier and lots more fun.

Don't be put off using a word because you don't know how to spell it. Have a go anyway. At least then you will get a better score for vocabulary and possibly persuasive devices and cohesion as well.

Coloured text is: Weaker level Standard level Stronger level

WRITING

COHESION
(and, but, so, however, on the other hand, another reason, since)

Scoring range 0–4

Weaker texts	Standard texts	Stronger texts
* Are short texts * Are missing cohesive links or have links which are wrong	* Include many sentences that are linked correctly * May use some simple synonyms e.g. bad, terrible, not good * Use pronoun references that are mostly correct	* Include most or all links that are correct * Allow the reader to easily follow the flow of ideas * Use synonyms for topic words e.g. home, habitat, haven, dwelling * Include a range of words and devices that are used to link sentences, ideas and paragraphs

Example texts:

Standard text

Spicy soups, crusty breads and best of all, mouth-watering desserts are just some of the delicious foods you could create if you learnt how to cook.

Without a doubt, cooking is a skill that everyone in our community should master. After all, food is one of the essentials for life. Although poor dietary choices and poor food hygiene also lead to many deaths each year from obesity and food poisoning. This is why the education that comes from learning how to cook properly is so important.

Learning to create tasty meals for friends and family is also a part of our way of life. When we gather for weddings, birthdays or other special occasions, how do we celebrate? Well with food of course!

So when someone in your family suggests you go out to grab a greasy hamburger for dinner, stop them and say, "How about we make our own?"

Stronger text

Spicy soups, crusty breads and best of all, mouth-watering desserts are just some of the delicious foods you could create if you learnt how to cook. But on the other hand should you bother?

It is clearly obvious to all that cooking is a skill that everyone in our community should master. After all, food is one of the essentials for life. Without it we die! How could you possibly argue the opposite?

Unfortunately poor dietary choices and poor food hygiene are creating new health issues in our community, as increasing numbers of people are becoming obese and developing related diseases such as diabetes. This is why the education that comes from learning how to cook properly is so important.

Learning to create tasty meals for friends and family is also a part of our way of life. When we gather for weddings, birthdays or other special occasions, how do we celebrate? Well with food of course!

So next time someone in your family suggests you go out to grab a greasy hamburger for dinner, stop them and say, "How about we make our own?" It is sure to be tastier, healthier and lots more fun.

Coloured text is: Weaker level Standard level Stronger level

PARAGRAPHS

(how you group your ideas, arguments and details)

Scoring range 0–3

Weaker texts	Standard texts	Stronger texts
* Do not use paragraphs OR * May have one block of text OR * Include random line breaks OR * Use a new line for each sentence	* Use paragraphs to separate introduction, body and conclusion * Have big sections of text * Include paragraphs that focus on one idea * Include at least 1 paragraph that has a topic sentence and some supporting detail	* Include paragraphs that have a topic sentence and some supporting detail * Are well organised and build up the text

The topic sentence is also known as the main idea. It is usually the first sentence in a paragraph.

Example texts:

Standard text

You wear one on a motor bike. You wear one riding a horse. But should you have to wear a helmet when riding a bike? Of course.

Helmets are worn on your head to protect it if you have an accident. They have foam on the inside to act like a cushion and a hard outer shell like a tortoise. If you have an accident and you are not wearing a helmet, then you could get badly hurt and have long lasting head injuries. Every year, hundreds of young children are admitted to hospital because they were not wearing a bicycle helmet when they fell off. Roads and footpaths are hard surfaces.

They might not be a popular fashion statement, but wearing a helmet might save your life. That is why they should be compulsory.

Stronger text

You wear one on a motor bike. You wear one riding a horse. But should you have to wear a helmet when riding a bike? Of course.

Helmets are an important safety accessory. They are worn on your head to protect it if you have an accident. Roads and footpaths are hard surfaces and they are unforgiving if you land on them with your head. Every year, hundreds of young children are admitted to hospital after road accidents because they were not wearing a bicycle helmet.

Unfortunately many helmets are not very fashionable. They have foam on the inside to act like a cushion and a hard outer shell, which makes the wearer look a bit like a tortoise. Local police officers often report warning young people about bicycle safety when their helmets are hanging off their handlebars instead of being on their heads. Your handle bars don't need protecting, but your head sure does!

Fashions come and go. But you only have one head and you need to look after it. That is why wearing a helmet when riding a bicycle should be compulsory.

WRITING

SENTENCE STRUCTURE

Scoring range 0–6

(this is all about the grammatical structure of a sentence – does it make sense?)

Weaker texts	Standard texts	Stronger texts
* Do not include complete sentences * Have very short text * Include some simple sentences that are correct	* Include simple sentences that are correct and some compound sentences that are correct * May have one or two complex sentences correct	* Most sentences of all types are correct OR * All sentences are correct but there is little variety

If you make a mistake with your verb form or a preposition, it is counted as a sentence error.

If you use a sentence using 'and' a lot, it will be an error.

At a score of 5/6 they may allow one small sentence error. A score of 6/6 means all are correct.

Examples:

Simple sentences	I don't like wearing a bicycle helmet. It looks silly. Bicycle helmets are an important safety item. You should wear one. You only have one head. You need to look after it.
Compound sentences	I would be happy to wear a helmet, but I don't like how they look. Helmets should be compulsory, so we can keep children safe. Helmets are an important safety item, yet so many children still don't wear one. You only have one head and you need to protect it. I don't like wearing a bicycle helmet because it looks silly.
Complex sentences	If helmets are not compulsory, then how will we keep children safe? That is why wearing a helmet when riding a bicycle should be compulsory. Helmets are worn on your head to protect it in case you have an accident. If you have an accident and you are not wearing a helmet, then you could get badly hurt and have long lasting head injuries.

To learn more about how to create complex sentences, refer to page 114 at the end of the writing section.

Coloured text is: Weaker level Standard level Stronger level

PUNCTUATION

Scoring range 0–5

(full stop, capital letter, comma, speech marks, dash, brackets, apostrophe ...)

Weaker texts	Standard texts	Stronger texts
* Have no evidence of punctuation OR * Minimal punctuation (capitals and most full stops) * Contain stray capital letters to begin words which are not proper nouns, or in the middle of words	* Contain most sentences with correct sentence punctuation and some examples of other correct punctuation * Have no stray capital letters * Include correct capitals for all proper nouns	* Contain correct sentence punctuation * Include almost all examples of other correct punctuation

Example texts:

Standard text

Cats and dogs are probably the most common household pet. But are they the best pet you can have?

Cats and dogs, even though they are cute furry little bundles when they are little, grow up to bite and scratch bark and poop. So many people get fed up with all the care these animals need and they end up dumping them in our National Parks for them to become feral. Miss wilson from the rspca said each year we have to put down hundreds of dogs and cats that were cruelly abandoned by their owners. It's awful, but there is no other way.

So what is the best alternative to a cat or a dog?

Well one animal you might not have thought of is the ferret. It's small and furry like a cat, but with the energy and playfulness of a dog. It will even eat your leftover dinner.

But when you think about it, the best pet anyone can have is a pet rock. No feeding, no messing and you don't even have to take it for a walk!

Stronger text

Cats and dogs are probably the most common household pet. But are they the best pet you can have? You might be surprised at which animal is actually the best pet!

Cats and dogs, even though they are cute, furry little bundles when they are little, grow up to bite and scratch, bark and poop. Many people get fed up with the care these animals need, and they end up dumping them in our National Parks for them to become feral. Miss Wilson from the RSPCA said, "Each year we have to put down hundreds of dogs and cats that were cruelly abandoned by their owners. It's awful, but there is no other way."

So what is the best alternative to a cat or a dog?

Well, one animal you might not have thought of is the ferret. It's small and furry like a cat, but with a dog's playfulness and energy. It will even eat your leftover dinner, so there's no need to worry about buying special food - great!

But when you think about it, the best pet anyone can have is a pet rock. No feeding, no messing and you don't even have to take it for a walk! Now that's what I call the perfect pet!

Coloured text is: Weaker level Standard level Stronger level

WRITING

SPELLING

Scoring range 0–6

Weaker texts	Standard texts	Stronger texts
* Do not include proper spelling (unless it is modelled words from the stimulus) OR * Less than 20 words written correctly * Include mostly simple words that are correct but there are mistakes with the spelling of common words	* All simple words and most common words are correct * Have a few difficult words correct	* Contain all simple, all common, and some difficult (10+) words that are correct * May have a few challenging words that are correct OR * If there are no challenging words, then correct spelling of at least 15 difficult words

Example texts:

Standard text

Cats and dogs are the most common household pets. But are they the best pet you can have?

Cats and dogs, even thow they are cute, furry little bundles when they are little, grow up to bite and scratch, bark and poop. So many people get fed up with all the care these animals need, and they end up dumping them in our Nashonal Parks for them to become feral. Miss Wilson from the RSPCA said, "Each year we have to put down hundreds of dogs and cats that were crooly abandond by their owners. It's orfull, but there is no other way."

So what is better than a cat or a dog?

Well, one animal is the ferret. It's small and furry like a cat, but with the energy and playfulness of a dog. It will even eat your leftover dinner.

But when you think about it, the best pet anyone can have is a pet rock. No feeding, no messing and you don't even have to take it for a walk!

Stronger text

Cats and dogs are probably the most familiar household pet. But are they the best pet you can have? You might be surprised at which animal is actually the best pet!

Cats and dogs, even though they are cute, furry little bundles when they are little, grow up to bite and scratch, bark and poop. So many people get annoyed with all the attention these animals need, and they end up dumping them in our National Parks for them to become feral. Miss Wilson from the RSPCA said, "Each year we have to put down hundreds of dogs and cats that were maliciously neglected or mistreated by their owners. It's appalling, but there is no other way."

So what is the best substitute to a cat or a dog?

Well, one animal you might not have given much consideration to is the ferret. It's small and furry like a cat, but with the energy and playfulness of a dog. It will even eat your leftover dinner.

But when you think about it, the best pet anyone can have is a pet rock. No feeding, no messing and you don't even have to take it for a walk!

Coloured text is: Weaker level Standard level Stronger level

Planning a persuasive text

One effective way of planning for your persuasive text, remembering you only have five minutes, is using a fishbone planner. This helps you think of some different arguments either for or against the issue, and then come up with some reasons or evidence to support them. Don't forget to try to think of some interesting and persuasive words to make you sound authoritative.

TOPIC:
Should school canteens be allowed to sell junk food?

NO

No. Children are becoming obese because of their poor diet.

No. Children are developing diseases like diabetes and heart disease.

No. Children get to eat junk food at birthday parties and other celebrations. They don't need it at school as well.

No. Children need to have a healthy diet so they can make the most of their learning at school. Junk food will interfere with their concentration.

YES

Yes. Children work hard at school and they deserve a special treat for their efforts.

Yes. School canteens make money from selling junk food and these profits go back to the school to buy books and other resources.

Yes. Children would still be eating junk food. They would just buy it from the corner shop or bring it from home.

Yes. Junk food nowadays is not as bad as it was. They are getting better food choices with less sugar and less salt that kids still enjoy.

Vocabulary lists for persuasive writing

When you are trying to persuade another person to agree with your point of view, you need to use special words. Often these words are powerful or emotive. They bring up strong positive or negative feelings. Using these types of words will help your score in the vocabulary section of the marking criteria. Also, if you learn how to spell the more difficult words, that will help you improve your spelling score as well. (See more about scores in the marking criteria section, pages 39–48)

Positive words	Negative words	Words to join/link ideas
brilliant	aggressive	and
handy	dreadful	so
valuable	terrible	if
support	ghastly	since
urgent	unfair	however
vital	ineffective	otherwise
unique	pressured	although
supportive	awful	on the other hand
dependable	penalise	because
improve	punishment	for example
incredible	deprive	as well as
crucial	frighten	also
certain	atrocious	firstly
obvious	spiteful	finally
confident	irritate	but
agree	error	given that
absolutely	conflict	as a result
must	irresponsible	while
secure	blunder	nevertheless
significant	decline	consequently

The persuasive writing begins

Once the five minutes planning time is up, you will have thirty minutes to write your text. Now that probably doesn't seem like a long time, so remember to concentrate on QUALITY and not just QUANTITY. However, you must remember to FINISH your text. A text without a conclusion may mean that you miss out on scoring some important marks. (See pages 39–48 for more about the marking criteria)

A scaffold (outline) for a persuasive text

Title: It should grab the attention of the reader and use strong emotive words.
Introduction: A few sentences (3–5) that tell the reader what the topic is, why it is an important issue, what your point of view on the issue is.
Body: A series of paragraphs. Each paragraph will have a few sentences. The first sentence of each paragraph will be the topic sentence. Each paragraph will have one new argument (for or against the issue) and reasons or evidence to support it.
Conclusion: A few sentences (3–5) that sum up (summarise) the main points of the issue and demand that the reader agree with you, or encourage them to take some form of action.

Writing a good title for a persuasive text

Now in NAPLAN, you don't get marks for the title itself, but you are scored on how well you engage your audience. The first part of your writing the audience reads is of course your title, so it needs to grab their attention and make them want to read what you have to say.

Look at some of these examples of titles for persuasive texts.

I don't like dogs

- Not very engaging
- Does give an opinion
- Identifies the topic
- Does not use powerful language
- Too personal

Homework - Children vs Parents

- More interesting with use of dash
- Introduces the topic of homework
- Shows that it will look at both side of the issue (vs)
- Identifies the points of view (children and parents)

HELP! Machines are controlling our lives!

- An interesting title because the reader will want to find out WHY and HOW
- Use of the word OUR brings the audience in to the text
- Powerful language appealing to the audience – HELP
- Use of exclamation marks for emphasis

Try this

The issue is: Should all children be made to play sport?

Create some interesting and powerful titles for your persuasive text.

____

____

____

A good title is short and to the point. It also helps to be inspiring or a bit controversial.

Getting a good start for a persuasive text

Persuasive text introductions need to be clear and summarise the main message. They must engage the reader and their emotions so that they want to keep on reading.

Some interesting ways to grab a reader's attention in persuasive texts are shown in the following examples.

Make sure you answer the rhetorical question in the body of the text.

Start the introduction with a rhetorical question such as:

What's the big deal about music videos?

Why do teachers waste so much time teaching handwriting?

Why on earth would anyone choose to smoke?

Write some rhetorical questions to start a persuasive text on the topic – **Art should not be taught at school.**

Try this

Start the introduction with highly emotive language such as:

Unfortunately, the local council has been ignoring the pleas of local residents to fix the intersection at Bradwell Drive, and this has led to disastrous results.

Quite clearly people in the local area are enraged with the irresponsible behaviour shown by disrespectful teenagers who choose to graffiti the new play equipment.

Use some emotive language (check out the word lists on page 50) to write the first sentence of an introduction to a persuasive text using the topic – **Sportsmen and women are paid too much.**

Personal pronouns are: I, we, us, our, you, my

Start the introduction by using personal pronouns to involve the reader such as:

I believe that it is vitally important to stop the hunting of whales in the South Pacific Ocean immediately.

You have got to be joking if you think that it's a good idea to ban school swimming carnivals!

Write a short introduction using personal pronouns to involve the reader in the issue on the topic – **School holidays should be shorter.**

Start the introduction with a clear statement of the topic such as:

Each year more of the world's rainforests disappear.

Politicians are often in the news for saying or doing the wrong thing, but they have a really important job to do.

Write an introductory statement using the topic – **Children should not be allowed to communicate over the internet.**

____

____

____

Try this

The body of a persuasive text

As you have seen, the body of your persuasive text is made up of several different paragraphs, each with its own argument and supporting reasons or evidence.

In the test, because there is a limited amount of time, you probably won't be able to write all the ideas you have. You will have to choose carefully which ones to use and which ones to leave out. Pick the arguments you believe in the most, and the arguments you can support with good reasons or evidence.

If you are writing an exposition (one point of view), then you will need about three paragraphs in your body. If you are writing a discussion (two different points of view) then you will probably need 3–4 paragraphs – two with arguments in favour and two with arguments against. Remember, if you have the time, of course you can write more. Let's have a look at one of these paragraphs for an exposition.

A short phrase to link this new paragraph with the topic and the introduction

The main idea – argument in favour

Reasons and examples to support the argument made at the beginning of the paragraph

To begin with, it is important for those people alarmed by the negative media coverage to understand that our climate has always been changing. In fact, it is one of the possible explanations for the extinction of the dinosaurs, millions of years ago. *Likewise*, the end of the ice age in prehistoric times was also due to the warming of Earth's climate. Both of these significant events occurred well before any human intervention. It is ridiculous to suggest that climate change is a modern catastrophe and that human actions are the only explanation.

Emotive words used to get the author's opinion across to the reader

Conjunction to link ideas within the paragraph

Now let's look at a paragraph from a discussion, where we are about to show a different point of view.

A connective to show a change in the point of view, but still keeping with the same topic

The main idea – argument against

Reasons and examples to support the argument made at the beginning of the paragraph

However, surely we cannot rule out the level of human involvement in climate change. Every day, factories vomit out huge amounts of toxic gas and other pollutants into the air we breathe. Coal fire power stations eject tonnes of carbon dioxide into the atmosphere. Governments know about this because they have started using air monitoring stations to work out where the worst spots are so they can try to do something to help.

Emotive words are used to get the author's opinion across to the reader

Evidence to support your arguments

To get the most out of your persuasive text, you not only need to tell the reader what is important about the issue, but also WHY it is important. You need to create links between your ideas and opinions and the arguments you are using to support them.

To do this you need SUPPORTING EVIDENCE.

But what does this supporting evidence (also known as reasons or details) look like?

Let's look at a simple statement or argument:

Topic: **Should children be allowed to play electronic games?**

Argument: Electronic games are bad for children.

How can we develop this argument, about electronic games being bad, and provide the reader with reasons why?

Here are a couple of examples.

Unfortunately children today seem to be obsessed with a wide variety of electronic devices from PlayStations to iPods. The way unsuspecting kids get sucked into these mindless games for hours and hours on end is terrifying. Whatever happened to playing outside with some friends or riding your bike at the park? Shooting hoops in basketball is certainly not as disturbing as the violent war games such as COD (Call of Duty) that our children are playing.

Add some extra persuasive words

Ask a rhetorical question directly to the reader

Give a real life example

It is shameful to see the amount of time children are spending playing electronic games. This time could be used more constructively by getting outside and being active, where they exercise more than just their thumbs! These video games are an addiction – just like smoking. Scientists who study the brain have found a concrete link between excessive use of video games and poor social skills. Is this what we want for our kids?

Use strong persuasive language

Give a variety of reasons to support the one argument

Use an 'expert' opinion to support your argument

Use strong persuasive language

Appeal to the values and emotions of the reader

Other supporting evidence

Facts and figures

* In a recent survey, over 85% of parents agreed that their children were obsessed with video and computer games.
* Most parents (3 out of 4) wanted children to spend less time on video games.
* Last year, children who played video games for less than 3 hours/week performed 35% better on their NAPLAN scores than children who played for more than 5 hours/week.

Expert Quotes

* Professor Dumblydorelatch said, "I have conducted my own studies in schools, and there is clear evidence to prove that video games decrease brain capacity."

Try this

Using the topic, create an argument and then work on developing a paragraph with reasons and supporting evidence.

Topic: Keep tourists out of our National Parks

Make your argument the topic sentence to start your paragraph.

Argument and supporting evidence:

Think about the words you use to link your ideas and reasons.

Think about the words you use to persuade the reader.

Check your spelling and use of correct punctuation. Can you use speech marks to quote an expert or bystander for evidence?

Persuasive devices

Below are some different ways you can reach out to your audience and persuade them to agree with a point of view. These tips are useful in the persuasive devices section of the marking criteria.

Appeal to logic and reason

- People who say cats make the best pets don't know what they are talking about.
- It is obvious that playing sport helps kids to be happier and healthier.

Use rhetorical questions

- What else are children expected to do if they aren't good at sport?
- People complain that children don't get outside and run around enough. Yet at school if they don't have a hat, they are forced to sit down. Is this fair?

Use comparison and contrast

- Many more boys are adversely affected by violent video games than their female classmates.
- While some adults agree that homework is important, many also complain about the amount of time it takes away from family life.

Reference statements

These are quotes from experts or a character involved with the topic. Normally, you would be expected to research your topic so that your quotes are true and accurate. However, in NAPLAN, you can't do any research so they will allow you to have a 'pretend' expert or quote from a character.

- Professor Mia Mumma said, "If governments continue to destroy our forests, then by 2035 there will be no rainforest vegetation left in Australia."
- "No way!" said Max, a 9-year-old video game fanatic, "I will never stop playing video games. They're my life!"

Appeal to values and emotions

- We all want to be healthy, but we still eat far too much junk food. That is why canteens should only sell healthy alternatives.
- We must stop bullying in schools. It's the right thing to do!

Use figurative language such as similes

- Computer games are <u>as addictive as</u> alcohol or tobacco.
- Their brains are like a bowl of mushy peas by the time they have finished spending hours playing video games.

Use of modality

Modality is where the level or intensity of a verb can be changed.

- You MUST do your homework – shows strong modality.
- You SHOULD do your homework – shows medium modality.
- You MIGHT do your homework – shows low modality

MODALITY	
LOW	may, can, could
MEDIUM	ought to, probably, might
HIGH	will, never, certainly

Writing a persuasive conclusion

In the NAPLAN writing task, your text will need a conclusion. It should:

- be in a separate paragraph
- summarise your most important arguments
- reinforce your point of view
- call for some type of action

A good conclusion will leave a lasting impression on the reader and, combined with the rest of the text, have them convinced that your point of view is correct.

POOR ENDING

So that is why we need to teach all children how to cook.

- Very short; it is only one sentence
- It does give a simple point of view
- What does 'that' mean?
- It does not summarise the main points

GOOD ENDING

Access to healthy food and a good education is a right for all children! By teaching students how to cook, we are reaching both goals at once. Children are reading, writing and using a wide range of mathematical skills at the same time as creating delicious food with fresh, healthy, Australian-grown produce. It can't get better than that!

- It summarises the main points
- It uses powerful language
- It appeals directly to the reader
- Statement with high modality

Try this

Using the topic of **Protect our National Parks** from page 57, write your own conclusion for a persuasive text.

____

____

____

Do not include new information in a conclusion.

If you need to change something, don't waste time rubbing it out – just cross it out and write the new word above it.

Don't worry if you cannot spell a difficult word. Use it anyway because it will help you get a better score in the vocabulary section.

The final edit for a persuasive text

Once your 30 minutes writing time is up, the teacher will tell you that you now have 5 minutes for editing. But if you haven't finished writing yet, don't worry; you can use some of the five minutes to complete your persuasive text. Remember, to score the most points in the structure section you must have a conclusion!

Revising and editing your work is an important part of the writing process. This is where you have a chance to check your work for any silly errors and maybe even add something to improve it.

Revision checklist

- Do you have a good title that includes the topic?
- Do you stay on the topic with all your ideas?
- Do you have a separate introduction that gives your point of view and uses some powerful words?
- Do all your sentences make sense?
- Have you used cohesive words and phrases to link your ideas between sentences?
- Have you used persuasive words throughout?
- Do you have each new argument in a separate paragraph with a reason or some supporting evidence?
- Do you have a conclusion to sum up your point of view and make a demand for action in a separate paragraph?

Editing checklist

- If you missed any paragraph breaks, use this symbol [to show where a new paragraph starts.
- Do all your sentences start with capital letters?
- Do all your sentences end with a full stop, exclamation mark or question mark?
- Do all proper nouns (names) begin with a capital letter?
- Have you accidentally put capital letters where they don't belong?
- Have you correctly used apostrophes for contractions? (e.g. don't, can't, isn't)
- If a person (expert) is talking, have you used speech marks?
- Have you spelt your words correctly?

Use the following stimulus materials to help you plan, write and edit your own persuasive text. It would be a good idea to have a timer so that you can practise in a similar environment to the real NAPLAN test.

Try this

Graffiti – is it art or vandalism?

What do you think about this idea? Write to persuade a reader to agree with your point of view.

Think about:

- if you agree or disagree or if you can see both sides of the topic
- an introduction – clearly say what you think about the topic
- your opinions – give reasons or examples to explain them and be persuasive
- a conclusion – a summary of your main points and a final comment on your opinion

Remember to:

- plan your writing before you begin
- make your writing interesting to read
- write in sentences and stay on the topic
- check your spelling and punctuation
- use words that will persuade your reader
- start a new paragraph for each new idea
- check and edit your writing when you are finished

Caged or Free – Should animals be kept in zoos?

What do you think about this idea? Write to persuade a reader to agree with your point of view.

Think about:

- if you agree or disagree or if you can see both sides of the topic
- an introduction – clearly say what you think about the topic
- your opinions – give reasons or examples to explain them and be persuasive
- a conclusion – a summary of your main points and a final comment on your opinion

Remember to:

- plan your writing before you begin
- make your writing interesting to read
- write in sentences and stay on the topic
- check your spelling and punctuation
- use words that will persuade your reader
- start a new paragraph for each new idea
- check and edit your writing when you are finished

NARRATIVE TEXTS

Narratives (a type of imaginative text) are also commonly known as stories and their main purpose is to entertain the audience.

As an author of a narrative text you may:

- tell the story from your own point of view (first person)
- tell the story as if you were watching it happen and not involved (third person)
- use humour or other emotions such as fear and sadness
- use a realistic or imaginative problem

It is easier to write about the actions of others and not put yourself in the story.

Types of narratives

There are many different genres of narrative writing. These include:

- Science fiction (Sci Fi)
- Mystery
- Horror
- Real life
- Detective – whodunnit
- Historical
- Myths and legends
- Fairy tales and folk tales

Depending on the information contained in the stimulus materials you are given, you may choose to use any of these genres in your narrative text.

It is easier to write in a genre that you enjoy reading yourself. It should also be a genre that you know about.

How will my narrative writing be marked?

The teachers who mark all the NAPLAN writing tests use the same marking criteria so no matter who you are, what your school is, or where you live, you are marked in the same way as everyone else.

The marking criteria have 10 different sections. Each section is marked separately, so if you don't do well in one section, you can still do well in all the others.

Narrative criteria summary

AUDIENCE (the people who will be reading the text) **Scoring range 0–6**

Weaker texts	Standard texts	Stronger texts
* Are very short * Are very simple * Copy the stimulus material * Use a simple title * Use a formula to begin 'Once upon a time'	* Use simple places and characters * Contain a consistent story that the reader can understand and follow * Contain a story that entertains * Try to use devices such as fantasy, sci fi and humour to engage the reader * Attempt to orient and engage the reader	* Use suspense and references to characters, events and settings from other texts * Tell a strong story * Engage the audience well

Example texts:

Standard text

Once upon a time in a land far, far away there was a Kingdom known as Sillybutt. It was ruled over by King Silly and his son Prince Crackle. Together they had managed to make a mess of just about everything. Instead of caring for the people, all they did was spend money on party clowns.

Every day as the people of Sillybutt went to work in the fields, they would complain about the King and his son. "Nothing ever gets done around here," said one man. "We pay our taxes to help the King get fat!" said another.

So one day, some of the palace servants went to a magician to ask for help. Pretending to be a clown at one of the palace parties, he put a spell on the King and his son that turned them into windup robots. So when the people of the Kingdom wanted anything done, all they had to do was wind up the King and away he went.

Now, the people of Sillybutt never had to worry about unfinished jobs again.

Stronger text

The cold, stone walls of the castle were keeping its secrets well hidden tonight. Flickering candles feebly tried to pierce through the darkness of the endless hallways.

Meanwhile, a lonely figure, dressed only a royal blue, dressing gown stumbled down the shadowy hallway, desperately searching for the porcelain treasure.

However, in his frantic haste, Sir Frederick Merryweather the Third had become hopelessly lost within the bewildering maze of corridors and libraries. His heart thundered in his chest, every heavy beat was a warning of the dreadful consequences if he was too late in finding the hidden treasure. His reputation would be ruined! He would be the laughing stock of the castle!

"Is anyone there?" he managed to croak through shallow breaths. "Pleeeaaase?" But his only answer was the icy wind whistling down the hallway. Even the castle seemed to be laughing at his predicament.

But, just as he thought all was lost, Sir Frederick spotted a small lamp flickering off to one side at the far end of the hallway. Yes! Finally he had found it! Disregarding all else, Sir Frederick barged headfirst through the door, whipped his dressing gown around him like a bullfighter's cape and promptly plonked his big, round bottom on the toilet seat.

"Aaahhh," he sighed. (Believe me you certainly don't want to know the rest!)

Coloured text is: Weaker level Standard level Stronger level

STRUCTURE (how the text is organised)		Scoring range 0–4
Weaker texts	**Standard texts**	**Stronger texts**
* Use the wrong text type * Use minimal structure * Have two structural sections – a beginning and a complication, but no ending * Recount events with no complication	* Have all three sections (orientation, complication and resolution) – but the ending may be weak (it was only a dream)	* Have details of events and may have more than one complication * May use flashback * Have an effective conclusion and/or coda * May have an unusual twist at the end

Always make sure you finish the text with a conclusion, even if it is only one or two sentences.

Example texts:

Standard text

Once upon a time, the Queen of Peggsville gave birth to a tiny, baby boy. She called him Peggsley.

As he grew up, Peggsley did all the normal things that young princes do. He rode horses. He played chess. He did archery. But Peggsley found life as a Prince to be boring. He wanted more adventure.

So one day, Peggsley decided that he was going to run away to find something more exciting to do with his life.

His father wished him luck. His mother cried. The palace servants laughed. But Peggsley left, ignoring them all and set off into the forest that surrounded the castle.

Later that same afternoon, Peggsley returned to the castle, covered in mud. "What on earth happened to you? And why are you back so soon?" demanded the King.

"Having an adventure is not as much fun as I thought," Peggsley replied. "So I have decided to stay being a Prince instead."

Over the following months, many people asked Peggsley what had happened in the forest, but he never told anyone.

Try to have a bit of a twist at the end to make your narrative different to the formula type endings of 'happily ever after' and 'it was only a dream'.

Try to be creative with your ideas. Be a little different.

Coloured text is: Weaker level Standard level Stronger level

Stronger text

Once upon a time, well before even your parents were born, high up in the stone-walled tower, Queen Wishy-Washy of Peggsville gave birth to a tiny, baby boy. In keeping with tradition of giving the first born son a name to remind him of his duty to the Kingdom, she called him Peggsley.

Now Prince Peggsley was a fine, upstanding young prince, loved by all in the kingdom. But it hadn't always been that way.

As he grew up, Peggsley did all the normal things that young princes do. He rode horses - but not very well. He played chess - but not very well. He did archery - but not very well. In fact, he was so bad at everything he tried that around the castle, Prince Peggsley became known as Prince Pipsqueak the Pathetic.

So one day, just before his tenth birthday, Peggsley decided that he had had enough of being teased and taunted for being weak. "I'm leaving home!" he informed his parents at breakfast.

The King shouted, the Queen cried, and the servants cheered as Prince Peggsley turned and walked out the door. "He won't be back," whispered the servants to each other. "He'll be eaten by wild bears or fall into a bottomless pit before the day is through."

Coloured text is: Weaker level Standard level Stronger level

IDEAS

(what you say in the text about the types of characters and events) **Scoring range 0–5**

Weaker texts	Standard texts	Stronger texts
* The ideas are not related to the topic * Have very few ideas * The ideas are very predictable (prince rescues princess from a dragon) * Does not include any detail	* Have a few ideas that have some details OR * One idea is well developed with good detail	* Have most ideas with relevant detail * Include a central story with a theme (good versus evil) * Include ideas such as a heroic quest or overcoming great odds to succeed

Example texts:

Standard text

Hooray! The biggest day of the year had finally arrived. "No more pencils, no more books!" chanted the year sixers as they headed off on their end-of-year excursion. Usually they went to the local water-play park, but last year, one of the teachers had ended up in the pool fully clothed, so this year they were going on a bushwalk. The teachers thought that would be less dangerous.

After a long and noisy bus trip south, year six arrived at Mount Slippery Slope National Park.

"Now children," announced the principal, Ms Obeyme, "Today is meant to be fun. We don't want any nasty accidents, so stay in the play area and please, don't go wandering off." But hardly anyone heard her as they went running around in all directions. And that is of course when it happened.

Thwack! Thud!

Rushing to get to the bag of sports equipment first, Arthur and Lancel managed to head butt each other.

Unfortunately, Ms Obeyme had a rather nasty habit of fainting at the sight of blood. So when she saw Arthur collapsed on the grass with blood dripping from his nose, she promptly joined him in a heap. Luckily for both Mrs Obeyme and Arthur, one of the other teachers, Mr B. Prepared, had thought to bring a first aid kit and he used his excellent emergency care skills on both patients while one of the other teachers rang for an ambulance.

Once Arthur and Mrs Obeyme were safely on their way to hospital, Mr B. Prepared and the remaining teachers decided that since the Principal was out of the way, that they too could enjoy themselves; after all - the picnic was to celebrate the end of the year. So they organised a mud pie fight with the year 6 students. You'll never guess who the winners were!

Not telling the reader everything and including a bit of mystery helps in writing a good narrative.

Coloured text is: Weaker level Standard level Stronger level

Stronger text

Just one more...

Each step got harder and harder for Josh as he neared the end of his endurance. Leaning exhausted against a hollow tree trunk he thought back to how he had gotten himself into this mess in the first place. Although really, when he thought about it, it wasn't all his fault.

Just this morning, he had been playing footy in the park with his mates, Boof, Sanga and Blue, but that seemed like a lifetime ago now. Boof had come up with the bright idea that because it was the holidays, they should do something. Sanga had thumped him on the back and said, "Playing footy IS something. No wonder we call you Boof!" The boys had cracked themselves laughing at that.

But then Dylan (the school bully) and his gang decided to butt in. "Hey, look at the little giggly girls," he taunted.

"We're NOT girls," Boof yelled back.

"We're just as tough as you!" they all shouted, sticking up for Boof. (That was their first mistake)

"Oh yeah?" said Dylan. "Then how about you prove it. Meet us down by the old, bush track this arvo and we'll see who's really tough."

So later that afternoon, Josh, Boof, Sanga and Blue met up at the old bush track behind the army grounds on their push bikes. Dylan and his gang were already there.

"Whatcha wearing helmets for girlies?" Dylan sneered. "Afraid you might hurt your pretty, little heads?"

The boys looked at each other and removed their helmets (their second mistake of the day).

"OK, you ready? First team down to Deadman's gully and back wins. Let's go!" Dylan shouted as he took off, not waiting to see if anyone else was ready.

Josh wiped his forehead with his arm. Ouch! He looked down to see a couple of deep scratches. "How did I get those?" he thought to himself. "Probably when I high sided over the handlebars after being side swiped by one of Dylan's boys. I should have known I couldn't trust them"

All Josh wanted to do was lie down and rest. Just a short one he promised. Just a few minutes to catch his breath. Slowly, he slid down the trunk until he collapsed in a heap on the ground and closed his eyes.

With a start, Josh woke! He was cold. Bitterly cold. It was dark. "Oh no!" Josh cried out. He had not meant for this to happen. It was night time and he still hadn't reached help. What would happen to Boof and Sanga, lying bloody and tangled on that rocky cliff edge now? Had he failed his friends when they needed him most?

Coloured text is: Weaker level Standard level Stronger level

WRITING

CHARACTER & SETTING
(the way you describe and present them through dialogue)

Scoring range 0–4

Weaker texts	Standard texts	Stronger texts
* Only give characters names or roles (dad, her brother) * Only give brief and simple descriptions (big, red, silly) * Include characters and/or setting are confusing to the reader	* May use simple or common similes * Attempt to develop a good understanding of the setting or the main character	* Give a very detailed description of character through dialogue, actions, interactions with other characters and thoughts * Include a setting that has an atmosphere which is maintained throughout the text

Interesting vocabulary will help you create better descriptions of your setting and characters.

Don't just describe how your character looks (brown hair, black boots, red coat). Describe the type of person they are – cheerful, shy and lonely, sly and sneaky. Describe how they talk and move as well.

Example texts:

Standard text

It was a cold, windy Friday night and nine-year-old Sarah was waiting for her dad to come home from his work in the city.

"Where is he, mum?" she asked for probably the tenth time.

"Don't worry, dear," said her mum. "You know dad, he probably stopped off to pick up the newspaper or something. He'll be home soon."

But Sarah wasn't so sure. The storm clouds were black and scary and you couldn't even see the moon. "What if something bad had happened? What if dad was in a bad crash?" Sarah thought.

Suddenly there was a loud thump outside on the front porch. Sarah ran. As she opened the door she let out a terrible scream, "Aarrgghhh!"

"Hey there chicken!" said her dad. "Why all the noise?"

"Oh dad, it's you," said Sarah as she gave her dad a great, big hug. That was when Sarah saw what was behind him and she screamed again. This time louder!

Stronger text

Thin curtains of wispy white dangled over the pale moon as Nikoli cautiously groped his way through the dense undergrowth. The forest was thicker here, almost as if it was trying to protect its secrets. But Nikoli was not going to let a few annoying obstacles stop him on his final quest. He had not come all this way for nothing.

Ever since he had been a young boy, growing up on the distant island of Cretina, his grandfather had entertained him with the most fanciful stories of the ancient Poonyah tribe and their long lost treasures. Grandfather had been an explorer and adventurer, and the tales of his many perilous journeys into the deepest jungles of South America were legendary, even now after he was gone.

Young Nikoli (who was yet to turn twelve) was determined to follow in his grandfather's footsteps. So when the opportunity arose, he became a stowaway on a boat headed for South America. Now, despite all the difficulties he had faced, he was almost within reach of his ultimate goal - the priceless treasure of the ancient and mysterious Poonyah tribe!

Coloured text is: Weaker level Standard level Stronger level

VOCABULARY (the types of words used) — Scoring range 0–5

Weaker texts	Standard texts	Stronger texts
* Are very short text * Have very few content words * Use mostly simple words – dragon, quick, really, very	* Use common similes – as black as night * May use a few precise words – snarled, hurtled, revolted	* Consistently use many precise words * Also use metaphor, personification, and interesting similes * Include writing that is fluent and articulate * Include vocabulary that is well matched to the genre (sci fi/ historical, mystery)

Example texts:

Standard text

"Come on Jessie!" I said, grabbing my little sister's hand. "We have to get inside before that storm hits!" I quickly looked over my shoulder to see the thick, rolling clouds coming closer. Within minutes that terrible storm would be here. It was going to be close.

Jessie could sense my fear. She was crying now. As the tears ran down her face, she reached up to wipe them away - and that was when she fell, pulling me down with her. "Oww!" she cried out.

"Stop complaining!" I yelled. "Get up. Come on...MOVE!"

"I can't," cried Jessie. "I think I've twisted my ankle." I leant over and had a quick look. Sure enough, Jessie's ankle was already starting to look puffy. I glanced towards the tornado shelter, it was so close! Then I looked back at the angrily approaching storm - it was even closer!

"Sorry," I said, "but this is going to hurt." And without waiting for Jessie to reply, I grabbed her underneath the armpits and started dragging her across the uneven ground towards the shelter.

Stronger text

"Come on Jessie!" I said, desperately grabbing my little sister's hand. "We have to get inside before that storm hits!" I nervously glanced over my shoulder just in time to see the thick, black glove snuff out the last rays of sunlight and it continued to move relentlessly towards us. It was going to be close.

Poor Jessie could sense my fear. She was crying now. As the salty tears ran down her face, she reached up to wipe them away - and that was when she fell, tumbling onto the hard packed earth, and dragging me down with her. "Oww!" she cried out in obvious pain.

"Stop whinging!" I snapped. "Get up. Come on... MOVE!"

"I can't," sobbed Jessie helplessly. "I think I've twisted my ankle." I leant over and had a quick look. Sure enough, Jessie's ankle was already starting to look like a squashed red tomato. I glanced towards the tornado shelter, it was so close! Then I looked back at the angrily approaching storm - it was even closer!

"Sorry," I muttered, "but this is going to hurt." And without hesitating, I seized her underneath the armpits and started hauling her across the uneven ground towards the shelter.

That was when catastrophe struck!

Don't be put off using a word because you don't know how to spell it. Have a go anyway, at least then you will get a better score for vocabulary and possibly characters, setting and cohesion as well.

Coloured text is: Weaker level Standard level Stronger level

COHESION

(and, but, so, however, meanwhile, later on, suddenly)

Scoring range 0–4

Weaker texts	Standard texts	Stronger texts
* Are short texts * Cohesive links are missed or wrong * May have one or two errors in pronoun referencing	* Include almost all sentences that are linked correctly * Include almost all pronoun references that are accurate	* Allow the reader to easily follow the flow of ideas * Use synonyms e.g. jump, leap, soar * Use conjunctions and connectives * Use a wide range of words and devices that are used to link sentences, ideas and paragraphs

Example texts:

Standard text

It was another day at school and as usual I had forgotten my homework. The bell rang and we all piled into class. Our teacher, Mr Doazyortold, stared at us.

"Has everyone handed in their homework assignment?" he asked, looking directly at me. My head drooped. "Where is your homework today, Lazenbutt?"

"Um, I'm sorry Mr Doazyortold," I murmured. "I... ah... don't actually have it."

"And why don't you have it, Lazenbutt?"

"Un, well, you see... my dog ate it!"

"But you don't have a dog, Lazenbutt!" Mr Doazyortold yelled. "Detention!"

So as you see, it was just another day at school.

Stronger text

Just one more...

Each step got harder and harder for Josh as he neared the end of his endurance. Leaning exhausted against a hollow tree trunk he thought back to how he had gotten himself into this mess in the first place.

Just this morning, he had been playing footy in the park with his mates, but that seemed like a lifetime ago now. Boof had come up with the bright idea that because it was the holidays, they should do something. Sanga had thumped him on the back and said, "Playing footy IS something. No wonder we call you Boof!" The boys had cracked themselves laughing at that.

But then Dylan (the school bully) and his gang butted in. "Hey, look at the little giggly girls," he taunted.

"We're NOT girls. We're just as tough as you!" they all shouted.

"Oh yeah?" said Dylan. "Then how about you prove it. Meet us down by the old, bush track this arvo and we'll see who's really tough."

So later that afternoon, Josh, Boof, Sanga and Blue met up at the old, bush track on their push bikes. Dylan and his gang were already there.

"Whatcha wearing helmets for girlies?" Dylan sneered. "Afraid you might hurt your pretty, little heads?"

The boys looked at each other and removed their helmets.

"OK, you ready? First team down to Deadman's gully and back wins. Let's go!" Dylan shouted as he took off.

The adventure that was to await them would turn out to be more than any of them had bargained for. If only...

Coloured text is: Weaker level Standard level Stronger level

PARAGRAPHS (how you group your ideas, arguments and details)		**Scoring range 0–3**
Weaker texts	**Standard texts**	**Stronger texts**
* Do not use paragraphs OR * Include one block of text OR * Random line breaks OR * A new line for each sentence	* Use paragraphs to separate broad changes in time and place (setting)	* Include paragraphs that focus on one idea * Are well sequenced to tell the story

Example texts:

Standard text

Many years ago, a little prince was born in the Kingdom of Peggsville. His parents called him Peggy.

Now life for Peggy in the castle wasn't easy. All the other princes teased him and made fun of him. He wasn't good at sport. He wasn't good at horse riding. He couldn't even master the royal wave. Poor Peggy wasn't good at anything! So one day he ran away. But when Peggy ran away, he found that life wasn't any better. No one bowed to him. No one called him 'Your Highness'. No one made his dinner, ironed his clothes or cleaned his room! Peggy was even more unhappy than before.

So one day Peggy decided that he would return home to the castle because that was where he belonged. And he did.

Stronger text

Once upon a time, the Queen of Peggsville gave birth to a tiny baby boy. In keeping with tradition of giving the first born son a name to remind him of his duty to the Kingdom, she called him Peggsley.

As he grew up, Peggsley did all the normal things that young princes do. He rode horses - but not very well. He played chess - but not very well. He did archery - but not very well. Around the castle, Prince Peggsley became known as Prince Pipsqueak.

So one day, just before his tenth birthday, Peggsley decided that he had had enough of being teased and taunted for being weak. "I'm leaving home!" he informed his parents at breakfast.

The King shouted, the Queen cried, and the servants cheered as Prince Peggsley turned and walked out the door. "He won't be back," whispered the servants to each other. "He'll be eaten by wild bears or fall into a bottomless pit before the day is through."

And do you know what? The servants were pretty close to the truth, for later that afternoon, a straggly figure stumbled back towards the castle. Yes, it was poor Prince Peggsley, covered from head to toe in dirt, leaves and foul smelling slime.

"What on earth happened to you? And why are you back so soon?" demanded the King.

"Well," said Peggsley, looking his father in the eye for the first time in his life, "being called Pipsqueak is nothing compared to being chased by wild bears, losing your pants in a slimy bog and having tree branches trying to scratch you face off. "

So it turned out that Peggsley was happy being a pipsqueak after all. I mean it would be boring if everyone was strong and brave, wouldn't it?

SENTENCE STRUCTURE — Scoring range 0–6

(this is all about the grammatical structure of a sentence – does it make sense?)

Weaker texts	Standard texts	Stronger texts
* Have no complete sentences * Are very short texts * Include some simple sentences that are correct	* Include most simple sentences that are correct and some compound sentences that are correct * May have one or two complex sentences correct	* Include most sentences of all types that are correct OR * All sentences are correct but there is little variety

If you make a mistake with your verb form or a preposition, it is counted as a sentence error.

If you use a sentence using 'and' a lot, it will be an error.

At a score of 5/6 they may allow one small sentence error. A score of 6/6 means all are correct.

Examples:

Simple sentences	One day I found a little box. It was sitting under a tree. I opened it. A funny creature jumped out. It ran around in circles. I said, "Stop!" The creature looked at me with its big, blue eyes. "No," it shouted. It ran away down the street.
Compound sentences	Once upon a time there was a King and he lived in a big castle on his own. The poor King was lonely because he didn't have any friends. One day a magician came to the castle so that he could entertain the King. "You had better make me laugh," warned the King, "or I will chop off your head!"
Complex sentences	Many years ago there was an old King who lived in a huge, golden castle all by himself. His name was King Rumblytummy and, as far as we know, he was a very kind King. When people came to him with their problems, King Rumblytummy would always lend a helping hand. If there were dragons causing havoc in the Kingdom, then the King would send his knights to destroy the beast and save the villagers.

To learn more about how to create complex sentences, refer to page 114 at the end of the writing section.

Coloured text is: Weaker level Standard level Stronger level

PUNCTUATION

Scoring range 0–5

(full stop, capital letter, comma, speech marks, dash, brackets, apostrophe ...)

Weaker texts	Standard texts	Stronger texts
* Have no evidence of punctuation OR * Minimal punctuation such as capitals to start sentences and full stops to end sentences * Include stray capital letters to begin words which are not proper nouns, or in the middle of words	* Include most sentences with correct sentence punctuation and some examples of other correct punctuation (such as commas, apostrophe for contractions, may have some correct speech marks but without correct commas to separate it from rest of text) * Include no stray capital letters * Include correct capitals for all proper nouns	* Include all sentence punctuation (capitals, full stops) that is correct * Have most examples of other punctuation that are correct (speech marks, dashes, brackets, commas, apostrophes)

Punctuation errors are not supposed to affect sentence errors. But poor punctuation can make it difficult to identify your intended sentences.

Example texts:

Standard text	Once upon a time, in a land far far away there was a kingdom known as Sillybutt. It was ruled over by King Silly and his son Prince Crackle. They tried their best, but together they had managed to make a mess of just about everything. Unfortunately they weren't very clever. Day after day the people of Sillybutt would complain about the King and his son. So one day when things were desperate some of the palace servants went to a magician to ask for help. He put a spell on the King and his son that turned them into windup robots. So when the people of the Kingdom wanted anything done all they had to do was wind up the King and away he went. After that the people of Sillybutt lived happily ever after!
Stronger text	Once upon a time, in a land far, far away there was a Kingdom known as Sillybutt. It was ruled over by King Silly and his son, Prince Crackle. They tried their best, but together they had managed to make a mess of just about everything. Unfortunately they weren't very clever and this made the King's servants frustrated. Day after day, the people of Sillybutt would complain about the King and his son. "Nothing ever gets done around here," grumbled one man. "We pay our taxes to help the King get fat! Why do we bother?" moaned another. No one was happy. So one day, when things were desperate, some of the palace servants went to a magician to ask for help. He put a spell on the King and his son that turned them into windup robots. So when the people of the Kingdom wanted anything done, all they had to do was wind up the King and away he went. After that, the people of Sillybutt lived happily ever after. (Thank goodness!)

Coloured text is: Weaker level Standard level Stronger level

SPELLING — Scoring range 0–6

Weaker texts	Standard texts	Stronger texts
* Do not include proper spelling (unless it is modelled words from the stimulus) OR * Include a few simple words correct (my, fun, must) OR * Include less than 20 words	* Include most simple words and some common words that are correct (again, their, wrong) * May have some difficult words correct (less than 10)	* Include all simple, all common, and some difficult (10+) words correct * May have a few challenging words correct

Invisibility and despicable are examples of challenging words.

Awful, invention, and enormous are examples of difficult words with many syllables.

The number of correctly spelt words must be more than the incorrect words to score at each level.

Example texts:

Standard text

It was a cold, windy Friday night and nine-year-old Sarah was waiting for her dad to come home from his work in the city.

"Where is he mum?" she asked for probbably the tenth time.

"Don't worry dear," said her mum. "You no dad, he probbably stopped off to pick up the newspaper or something. He'll be home soon."

But Sarah wasn't so sure. The storm clouds were black and scarey and you couldn't even see the moon. "What if something bad had happend? What if dad was in a bad crash?" Sarah thort.

Suddenly there was a loud thump outside on the front porch. Sarah ran. As she opened the door she let out a scream, "Aarrgghhh!"

"Hey there chicken!" said her dad. "Why all the noyse?"

"Oh dad, it's you," said Sarah as she gave her dad a great big hug. That was when Sarah saw what was behind him and she screamed agen. This time louder!

Stronger text

Thin slivers of moonlight danced merrily between the branches as Nikoli carefully groped his way through the dense undergrowth. The forest was thicker here, almost as if it was trying to protect its mysterious secrets. But Nikoli was not going to let a few scratches and bruises stop him on his quest. He had not come all this way for nothing.

Ever since he had been a young boy, growing up on the distant island of Cretina, his grandfather had told him stories of the marvellous treasures of the almost forgotten Poonyah tribe. Grandfather had been an explorer and adventurer, and the stories of his many dangerous journeys into the deepest jungles of South America were legendary.

Nikoli was determined to follow in his grandfather's famous footsteps. So once he was of age, he stowed away on a boat headed for South America. Now, despite all the difficulties he had faced, he was almost within reach of his ultimate goal – the priceless treasure of the ancient and mysterious Poonyah tribe!

If you use a correct difficult word more than once ('treasure' in the example text) then it is only counted once.

Coloured text is: Weaker level Standard level Stronger level

Planning a narrative text

One effective way of planning for your narrative text is to make a story path or story map. Remember you only have 5 minutes to plan, so it is important to get these ideas down (along with some interesting words).

- Who will my characters be?
- Where will my story take place?
- How will it begin?
- What will the problem be?
- How will the problem be solved?
- What will my title be?

In NAPLAN, you will be given a blank piece of paper for your planning page. Do not plan on your test booklet.

Title: *Strange noises*
Characters: *Mark, his friend Wendy, Mark's mum and the man next door*
Setting: *An ordinary suburb.*

Mark's best friend moves away because his dad got a new job. A new neighbour moves into the house. The man seems a bit strange and keeps to himself.

Mark becomes concerned when he hears strange noises coming from the man's garage – even when it is late at night. But his mum won't listen to him.

One day, Mark rides past the man's house on his skateboard. For some reason, the man won't look at him. He runs away and hides in the garage.

The following day, Mark realises that his skateboard has gone missing. He blames the man across the road for stealing it.

Mark and his friend Wendy try to catch the man. They sneak up to his house one night with a camera, trying to take photos of what is in his garage.

The man catches them and calls Mark's mum. She explains that the man is a retired mechanic and he was repairing the skateboard as a surprise, since Mark's mum can't afford to buy a new one.

Vocabulary lists for narrative texts

When writing your NAPLAN narrative, the words you choose to use are very important. They can affect your scores in:

- vocabulary
- cohesion
- character and setting

Words for speech

whisper	demand
softly	grumble
mutter	sigh
loudly	moan
yell	groan
angrily	roar
scream	growl
sadly	whimper
shout	order
kindly	bellow
whine	quietly
gently	complain
mumble	calmly
noisily	argue

Words for movement and action

crawl	sleepily	squeeze
hide	carefully	grab
scuttle	slowly	trample
slide	sneakily	deeply
barge	carelessly	tightly
burst	quickly	scamper
hurry	crash	haul
hurtle	plunge	evacuate
spoil	creep	flee
warning	slither	quickly
explode	shrink	cleverly
suddenly	swoop	silently

Figurative language is the creative way writers use the sound and meaning of words to describe.

Figurative language

Similes	Metaphors	Personification
He stood before the angry principal, quivering like a bowl full of jelly. The criminal tiptoed down the hallway as quietly as a mouse. The tornado created havoc like a runaway vacuum cleaner. The children squealed like baby piglets.	The police officer glared at him with a wooden face. (looking without emotion) Serena was the shining star at the end-of-year concert. The princess had a heart of gold. (kind and caring, priceless) The big, black dog was heavy on his shoulders. (being depressed) A torrent of lies fell from his mouth as he tried to find a good excuse.	The coffee grinder ate its meal and then spat it out. The tornado picked up the cars and tossed them away. The sleaves danced in the summer breeze. The ocean spray tickled my skin. The dark corners of the cave beckoned me closer.

Words and phrases to link ideas and events	
Later on	As they were leaving/ walking/talking
After that	Almost immediately
Finally	A little while later
Meanwhile	In next to no time
Soon	Unexpectedly
Before	Out of the blue
Shortly	Without notice
Suddenly	To begin with
Then	The following afternoon
Now	All of a sudden
One day	Throughout the day
During	
At last	
Before long	

Words to describe characters and/or settings	
timid	cuddly
elegant	grimy
shy	annoying
ferocious	selfish
enormous	angry
grumpy	greedy
hairy	bad-tempered
honest	wild
red-headed	brave
miserable	dangerous
loud	boastful
playful	helpful
excited	careless
powerful	lumpy
nervous	cranky
lonely	nasty
adorable	eager
secluded	wicked
cute	revolting

The narrative writing begins

Once the five minutes planning time is up, you will have thirty minutes to write your text. Now that probably doesn't seem like a long time, so remember to concentrate on QUALITY and not just QUANTITY. However, you must remember to FINISH your text. A narrative without an ending or resolution may mean that you miss out on scoring some important marks. (See pages 63–74 for more about the marking criteria)

A scaffold (outline) for a narrative text

Title: (that grabs the attention of the reader and tries to create a sense of atmosphere)
Orientation: (also known as the introduction) This is where the setting is established and the main characters are introduced with perhaps some background information about them or an event that will lead up to the complication later. A more advanced style of narrative includes a flashback, where the story begins after the problem has been resolved, and takes the reader back to how it all began.
Complication: In a good narrative, you will have one or two events that happen before the complication. The complication is where something goes wrong – there is a problem to be solved. In a more detailed narrative, there may be more than one complication.
Resolution: (also known as the ending or conclusion) This is where someone, usually the main character, tries to solve or fix the problem.
Coda: (this is optional) A coda is the moral, message or meaning to the story. It is where the characters learn something about themselves, or where there is a message to the reader about how to behave.

Writing a good title for a narrative text

Now in NAPLAN, you don't get marks for the title itself, but you are scored on how well you engage your audience. The first part of your writing the audience reads is of course your title, so it needs to grab their attention and make them want to read what you have to say.

Look at some of these examples of narrative titles.

The Dragon

This is a standard title that tells us the main character but not much else. There is no sense of expectation or interest about what might happen in the story.

The unusual neighbour

This is a bit more interesting. There is a sense of the reader asking 'Who is this neighbour?' and 'Why are they unusual?' This makes the reader want to find out.

Oh No - Meredith!

This is another good title. It uses a dash, so makes use of more advanced punctuation. The reader wants to read the story to find out what Meredith did.

Use the title to grab the interest of the reader. But it must match your story well.

Getting a good start to your narrative text

The main purpose of a narrative is to entertain. So if your story has a boring or slow orientation, it is unlikely that the audience will want to keep reading. In NAPLAN, it is really important that your narrative gets off to a good start, so that you can develop the description of your characters and setting, and have interesting ideas and events leading up to your complication.

Remember, the orientation (introduction) for your narrative must tell the reader:

1. when
2. where
3. who

There are a number of different ways to start a narrative:

1. Use dialogue to introduce the reader to the characters in a very personal way.

"All right class! Quiet now!" called Mrs Cauldron, clapping her hands briskly. "Misha Broome, what on earth are you trying to do?" she queried in an exasperated tone. For poor Misha was one of the worst students at The Witches Academy for Young ladies.

- By using dialogue you can start describing your characters through actions as well as speech. It shows how they interact with others.
- You also get right into the story without wasting time with unnecessary detail.
- By using direct speech, you can also help raise your scores in punctuation.

Try this

Imagine you are writing a story about a boy whose little brother comes into his room and ruins his science homework project. Write some dialogue to begin your narrative.

2. Use a few interesting sentences that take the reader straight into the action.

Tick...tock...tick...tock... Time was slipping away. Marcus could feel the icy, cold hands of fear slowly creeping closer and closer. They wanted him - only him.

- By using sentences like this, it creates a bit of mystery for the reader. What is Marcus doing? Who wants him? Why do they want him?
- You also get the chance here to use language features such as metaphors and personification to boost your vocabulary scores.
- The use of ellipsis and dashes also help to boost your punctuation scores.

Imagine you are writing a story about a sporting team (soccer, footy, basketball etc) who are playing in the Grand Final. Write some interesting sentences to begin your narrative.

____

____

____

Try this

3. Use a description of the setting to create clear images of the scene and the atmosphere in the mind of the reader.

The Valley of the Lost was a perfect name for this place, thought Eli as he looked around at the tangled branches and overgrown brush. It would be easy to get lost here. Barely a scrap of daylight was able to penetrate the thick, green canopy of leaves and vines that threatened to ensnare the unwary traveller.

- By using a description like this, you help to create an interesting atmosphere which engages the reader. This is great for doing well in characters and setting.
- You also get the chance here to use language features such as similes and personification to boost your vocabulary scores.

Imagine you are writing a story about a group of friends who go off on their own whilst on a school excursion. Write a description of the setting to begin your narrative.

____

____

____

____

Try this

When you are writing a narrative, creating an interesting setting is really important. If your setting is weak, it is like watching a movie with no background – just a blank wall.

4. Introduce the main character so that the reader can identify with him or her. Remember to include some detail about their personality.

Garth was not your usual blood-sucking, bone-crunching type of giant. He didn't grunt when you spoke to him. He didn't bathe only once a year when it rained. Garth was quite unusual, and when you're living with a pack of 'normal' giants, this can be quite a problem.

- By using a description like this, you help to create a character the reader can understand.
- You also get the chance here to use language features such as adjectives.
- You also get the chance to use punctuation such as apostrophes for contractions and commas to separate ideas in a sentence.

Try this

Imagine you are writing a story about a boy whose little brother comes into his room and ruins his science homework project. Write a description of one of the characters to begin your narrative.

____

____

____

____

____

The way to make characters seem real to the audience is to use a combination of description, dialogue, action and interaction with other characters.

HINTS FOR DESCRIBING CHARACTERS

- Appearance
  Wrinkles like a crumpled shirt
  Brown leathery skin
  Tall and skinny like a beanpole
- Personality
  Withdrawn, lonely, isolated
  Sunny, friendly, cheerful, positive
  Angry, hostile, difficult
- Personal history
  Recently moved house
  Often gets in trouble at school
  Has been bullied before
  Hates being compared to her older sister

Writing a good complication for a narrative text

Once you have an interesting introduction, where you have established the atmosphere (setting, time and place) and introduced the main characters, then you are ready to start moving into the complication stage of your narrative. This is where something goes WRONG.

It is important to remember not to jump straight into the problem. A good narrative, one that appeals to the audience, has one or two minor events which lead up to the real complication. This extra detail will allow you to continue to develop the description of your setting and characters, make interesting vocabulary choices and enhance the overall structure of your narrative.

A complication is a problem that needs to be solved e.g. someone is lost in a spooky forest with wild animals.
A complication is NOT a disappointment e.g. I dropped my ice cream on the ground.

Take, for example, the following narrative about *The Mystery of Wolli Creek*.

Upper Wolli Creek wasn't much of a town. In fact, it wasn't a town at all, just a haphazard collection of timber shanties and, of course, a pub. Freezing cold in winter, and so hot in summer it would melt the tar on the road, Wolli Creek only had one thing going for it - opals. For hundreds of kilometres, people came to find their fortune. But as it turned out, they got more than they bargained for... ← orientation

"That's my eleventh patient this week!" complained Doc Roberts. "Fever, delirium, night sweats. I wish I knew what was causing it." ← event leading to the complication

"Probably May's cooking. I swear that pork roast I had at the pub last week wasn't pork, probably road kill roo," replied Bluey Mason.

"I know what you mean," said Doc. "But I'm afraid you're barking up the wrong tree Bluey. I'd already thought of that but it came up clean as a whistle. I'm working on another theory though. Maybe you could help?" ← more details about the event

Doc pulled Bluey in close and explained what he wanted him to do. "Are you sure?" queried Bluey. "Well I never..." ← event

Meanwhile, in the dining room of May's pub, the locals were holding a town meeting. They were becoming increasingly concerned by the mystery illness sweeping through their small community. ← complication

Try this

Asteroid Attack!

Three computer games programmers enter the world inside their computer.

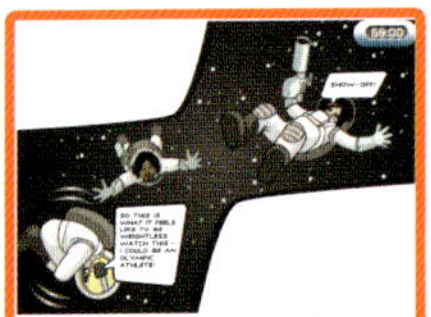

They find themselves floating in space. The boys do tricks in zero gravity.

Suddenly they see a huge asteroid that is headed straight towards them.

They fire a rocket at the asteroid.

The asteroid explodes, but it sends two of the friends spinning deeper into space!

Use this series of events to write the rest of the complication for this narrative. What will happen?

____

____

____

____

____

Writing a good complication for a narrative text

There are four things you need to tell your audience about when writing your complication:

1. What went wrong
2. When it went wrong
3. Who was involved
4. Why it went wrong

Things to remember

The series of events and the complication are probably going to be the biggest part of your NAPLAN narrative, so it is important that you do a few things well.

1. Keep using interesting words to describe what your characters do and how they do it.

Working as quickly as I dared, for stealth is of utmost importance when dealing with buried treasure, I delved into the nearest pile of debris.

As Fox was relaxing by the edge of an ice hole, Brown Bear came ambling up to his friend.

The frightened group huddled together under the flimsy shelter, desperately trying to maintain hope of a rescue.

2. Try to use a little direct speech, where at least one of your characters talks. This means you then have the opportunity to boost your punctuation score.

"Wh...wh...who is it?" he enquired timidly.

The Captain's piercing blue eyes surveyed the deck.
"I thought I told you to clean up this pigsty. Get to it, or there'll be no supper tonight."

Derek, covered in dirt and grime, stared at the monster. "Is that all you've got?" he demanded in disbelief. "My little sister can roar louder than that!"

3. Sequence the events using conjunctions and good sentence starters.

For the time being, they were safe. But for how long?

As the sun began the slow dip below the horizon, the strange humming noise started up again.

The following day, life went on as usual. It was almost as if it had never happened.

Resolving your narrative texts

This is an important part of the structure for a narrative. It is where the problem is solved. It is important to remember that a weak resolution (such as 'I woke up and it was just a dream' or just sticking 'They lived happily ever after' at the end without any explanation) will not score you full marks for structure.

A good resolution solves the problem from earlier in the story. It tells the reader:

1. When the problem was solved
2. Who solved the problem
3. How the problem was solved
4. What happened when the problem was solved

Look at the following example.

Complication: Ming Ming had been sent to collect some tasty herbs for an important dinner. But she spent her time day dreaming and broke her mother's special carry basket. Now she wouldn't be able to carry the herbs home. How was this problem resolved?

As Ming Ming sat weeping on the path, she looked up and saw a strange carving on a tree. She moved closer to read it: "the longest journey starts with a single step." Ming Ming wiped her face and made a decision. Her mother was relying on her. She did not want her family to lose face. She must find a solution.

Searching the nearby area, she found some hollow seed pods and used them to carry the herbs that she needed.

when the problem was solved

who solved the problem

why the problem needed to be solved

how the problem was solved

Ending your narrative text

The ending of your story is the last chance you have as a writer to leave a good impression on your audience. Sometimes it is easy just to say the problem is solved and that is the end (Ming Ming found the herbs and took them home in the hollow seed pods.). But a good ending has something more for the audience. It looks at what happened after the problem was solved.

When Ming Ming finally made it back to the village, her mother was anxiously waiting. Quickly Ming Ming recounted her story. Her father overheard the tale and his heart swelled with pride. He praised his daughter for her clever thinking and she was treated as an honourable guest during the evening meal.

Other effective ways to end your narrative after the resolution

With a question
"It's alright. You're safe now," mum whispered softly in my ear as she held my shivering wet body close to hers. Yes, I was safe; for now. But what would have happened if mum had been just five minutes late?

With an exclamation
Well today certainly didn't go according to plan. But I was not ready to give up just because of one failure. I was determined to get back at Jake, no matter what!

With a cliff hanger (the start of a possible new complication, after the one in your story has been solved)
Dad gratefully put 'How to be a vampire' back on the book shelf. I guess, like me, he had had enough of being chased by black cloaked fangs around the house. Just then, Mum came home. "This place is a mess!" she said. "What on earth have you two been up to?" Dad and I just looked at each other and raised our eyebrows. "Well never mind. I'll clean it up tomorrow. But look what I bought you darling," she said handing me a package. "It's a new book 'How to be a Ghoul'. Maybe Dad can read it to you tomorrow night?"

The final edit

Once your 30 minutes writing time is up, the teacher will tell you that you now have 5 minutes for editing. But if you haven't finished writing yet, don't worry; you can use some of the five minutes to complete your narrative text. Remember, to score the most points in the structure section, you must have a good resolution! Revising and editing your work is an important part of the writing process. This is where you have a chance to check your work for any silly errors and maybe even add something to improve it.

Revision checklist:

- Do you have a good title that interests the reader?
- Do you stay on the topic with all your ideas?
- Do you have a separate orientation that introduces the setting and main characters?
- Do all your sentences make sense?
- Have you used cohesive words and phrases to link your ideas and events between sentences?
- Have you used interesting and descriptive words throughout?
- Do you have each new event or setting in a separate paragraph with some supporting details?
- Do you have a complication where something goes wrong?
- Do you have a strong resolution where the main characters try to solve the problem?
- Have you given your story an ending?

If you need to change something, don't waste time rubbing it out – just cross it out and write the new word above it.

Editing checklist

- If you missed any paragraph breaks, use this symbol [to show where the paragraph begins.
- Do all your sentences start with capital letters?
- Do all your sentences end with a full stop, exclamation mark or question mark?
- Do all proper nouns (names) begin with a capital letter?
- Have you accidentally put capital letters where they don't belong?
- Have you correctly used apostrophes for contractions? e.g. don't, can't, isn't
- If a character is talking, have you used speech marks?
- Have you spelt your words correctly?

Don't worry if you cannot spell a difficult word. Use it anyway because it will help you get a better score in the vocabulary section.

Use the following stimulus materials to help you plan, write and edit your own narrative text. It would be a good idea to have a timer so that you can practise in a similar environment to the real NAPLAN test.

Try this

THE EXPERIMENT

Today you will be writing a narrative. This is also known as a story.

Your story might be about a science project at school, a time travel device, a mad scientist or even cooking a new dish for dinner.

THE DOOR

Your story might be about finding something unusual or spooky behind the door, discovering something old that brings back memories, or the door might be a portal into another world or time. It could also be about mysterious events that happen when you open the door.

You need to think about:

- the characters and the setting (time and place)
- the complication or problem to be solved
- how the story will end

Remember to:

- plan your story before you begin
- write in sentences and paragraphs
- use interesting words, and be careful with your spelling and punctuation
- check and edit your writing at the end

INFORMATIVE TEXTS

Use any stimulus pictures to help you with organising your information into paragraphs.

Informative texts are written to give the audience information – facts and data.

As an author of an informative text you should write:

- from an 'expert' point of view using third person (it, they, their)
- without using personal opinions and personal experiences
- using technical words related to the topic
- in a logical sequence of ideas or steps

Types of informative texts include:

- information reports (including social and scientific reports)
- procedures such as instructions and directions
- recounts
- explanations
- news articles
- biographies

The stimulus material will tell you which type of informative text you will need to use. Since the same material is used in NAPLAN for grades 3, 5, 7 and 9 it is likely to be a text type such as an explanation or scientific report.

Stick to the important facts. If the topic is dinosaurs, DO NOT write about when you went to the museum to see the dinosaur skeletons with your parents.

How will my informative writing be marked?

The teachers who mark all the NAPLAN writing tests use the same marking criteria so no matter who you are, what your school is or where you live, you are marked in the same way as everyone else.

The marking criteria have 10 different sections. Each section is marked separately, so if you don't do well in one section, you can still do well in all the others.

Informative text criteria summary

AUDIENCE (the people who will be reading the text)		Scoring range 0–6
Weaker texts	**Standard texts**	**Stronger texts**
* Are very short * Are very simple * Use a simple title * Copy the stimulus material * Use personal comments instead of factual information	* Use an interesting title * Provide a range of detail on different areas/stages of the topic * May use generic 'we', 'you' to help relate to the audience. E.g. You think all cows are the same but... * Are easy for the reader to follow and understand	* Engage the audience well * Use a sense of authority

Example texts:

Standard text	The Human Eye The human eye is a very important part of our body. Without it, you could not see. Light hits the front of the eye and goes into the eye through the pupil. When it is really sunny, the pupil gets smaller and when it is dark the pupil gets bigger. Also at the front of the eye is a lens. You use that to focus on things so they are not blurry. If your lens doesn't work properly, you might have to wear glasses. When the light goes through the eye, it gets to the retina and the signal is sent from the nerve at the back to the eye to the brain. The brain then tells you what you are looking at.
Stronger text	Looking through your eyes The human eye and its components operate almost in the same way as a movie camera. Each part needs to work at its best to provide a person with a clear window to the world. To begin the process, light hits the front of the eye, the cornea, which then bends the rays and directs them through the pupil, which is a dark circular opening at the centre of the coloured iris. High levels of light make the pupil dilate, while low levels of light make it expand. Because the cornea is curved, and the rays of light are bent, the image sent to the brain is upside down. It is eventually righted by the brain. Behind the cornea is the lens which is able to change shape so that it can focus on objects close up or at a distance. When people suffer an affliction known as cataracts, the lens becomes cloudy and needs to be replaced by an artificial or donor implant. Once through the lens, the light hits the back wall of the eye, a thin membrane known as the retina. Here, the light signals are changed into electrical impulses and sent along the optic nerve to the brain which then interprets these signals as visual images.

Coloured text is: Weaker level Standard level Stronger level

STRUCTURE (how the text is organised)		Scoring range 0–4
Weaker texts	**Standard texts**	**Stronger texts**
* Use the wrong text type * Have minimal structure – a beginning only or different aspects of the topic mixed up * Are just a series of statements	* Have two structural sections – an introduction and a body, or a body and a conclusion * Include an introduction that may be contained in the first sentences and may not be in a separate paragraph * May have an introduction and a conclusion but one is weak * Include details about 3 different aspects/stages of the topic in the body	* Have all three sections (introduction, body and conclusion) * Have an introduction and conclusion separate from the body * Have all three sections that are well developed * Include facts and details about four or more aspects or stages of the topic

The introduction to an informative text must classify the topic or identify what will be explained.

A title is not included as part of the structural score. It is not counted as an introduction.

Example texts:

Standard text

Milking Cows

The first step is for the cows to eat grass. The grass is chewed and goes into stomach 1 - the rumen.

Then the grass goes into stomach number 2 - the reticulum, where it is made into small lumps. These lumps are regurgitated back into the cow's mouth to be chewed some more.

Once each lump is chewed, they are swallowed and go into the third stomach - the omasum, and then it goes into the fourth stomach - the abomasum. From here, the nutrients from the grass go to the udder to make milk.

In order for cows to make milk, they need to drink lots of water. Cows also need to be milked regularly to make sure they keep producing more milk for us to drink.

Even though some informative texts don't actually have a separate conclusion like persuasions and narratives, still try to include a final statement to complete your text.

Coloured text is: Weaker level Standard level Stronger level

Example texts:

Stronger text	Turning Grass into Milk Did you know that not all cows can produce milk? Only cows that have given birth to a calf can make milk and even then, the process takes about 60 hours. The first step is for the cows to eat grass. It is important for them to eat a variety of grasses to get the proper range of nutrients to make good quality milk. This grass is not chewed properly before it is swallowed and stored in the first of a cow's four stomachs, the rumen. Fluids in the rumen soften and break down the hard stalky cellulose in the grass. Once this occurs, the grass is transferred to the second stomach, the reticulum. Here it is made into small lumps called 'cuds' which the cow regurgitates back into the mouth before chewing them for a second time. Each cud is chewed for about one minute. They are then swallowed into the omasum, the third of the cow's stomachs, where the process of softening and breaking down the grass continues. The final stomach is called the abomasum where the grass is digested. Then it moves into the intestines where the cow absorbs all the nutrients it needs to keep healthy. Whatever is left over goes to the udder to be made into milk, or leaves the body as waste. In order for cows to make milk, they need to drink lots of water, almost 100 litres per day. Cows also need to be milked regularly, to make sure that they keep producing 4,500 litres of milk each per year.

Coloured text is: Weaker level Standard level Stronger level

IDEAS (what you say in the text – your facts and details)		Scoring range 0–5
Weaker texts	**Standard texts**	**Stronger texts**
* Have one idea with simple details OR * The ideas are not related to the topic OR * A few ideas are related to the topic with very basic details	* Have one idea that is well developed with good detail OR * Most ideas have relevant detail	* Include ideas that are very informative * Include ideas that explain cause and effect * Are organised in a coherent way * Include ideas that are highly relevant

Example texts:

Standard text

Throughout the world there are lots of types of crocodiles but there are only two types of alligators. They can both be quite aggressive, but the crocodile is known to be more aggressive.

Alligators and crocodiles are both reptiles. Crocodiles have long, thin V-shaped snouts whereas alligators have short flat U-shaped snouts (a bit like a shovel). The crocodile also differs from the alligator in that when its mouth is closed, the fourth tooth is seen outside the mouth. The alligator has webbed feet, while the crocodile has clawed feet, even though they both spend most of their time in the water.

Many years ago, alligators and crocodiles were hunted for their skin. Now, in Australia, the Estuarine crocodile is protected and is only hunted when it poses a danger to people.

Stronger text

Throughout the world there are over 8700 known species of reptiles. One family of reptiles is the crocodilians, made up of crocodiles and alligators. There are several species of crocodiles throughout the world (including the Estuarine, Nile, Philippine and Mugger); however, there are only two species of alligators (American and Chinese).

Just like other cold blooded reptiles, crocodiles and alligators also need to keep their body temperature steady. So they are often found basking in the sun during cool weather and resting in the shade when it is hot. Temperature is also critical to crocodilian reproduction. If a clutch of eggs is incubated at less than 30 degrees Celsius, all of them will be born female. While if the temperature goes above 33 degrees, the clutch will be born all male.

Crocodiles have long, thin V-shaped snouts whereas alligators have short flat U-shaped snouts (a bit like a shovel). The crocodile also differs from the alligator in that when its mouth is closed, the fourth tooth is seen outside the mouth.

Another interesting difference between the two massive reptiles is that the alligator has webbed feet, an adaptation to help it move through the water; whereas, the crocodile has no webbing, just clawed feet.

Because of their aggressive nature, and the fact that their skin is useful in making leather for shoes and handbags, many species of crocodilians have been ruthlessly hunted. In Australia, the Estuarine crocodile is protected and is only hunted when it poses a danger to people.

Coloured text is: Weaker level Standard level Stronger level

DESCRIPTION AND DETAILS

Scoring range 0–4

(the way you describe your information about the aspects/stages of the topic)

Weaker texts	Standard texts	Stronger texts
* Are very short texts * Do not have a developed description (only single adjectives used e.g. big beaks) * Have little or no elaboration of ideas	* Use multiple adjectives to describe an aspect e.g. An owl has big round eyes * Use two different descriptive strategies (as listed below) in addition to the use of adjectives	* Use interesting similes e.g. A pelican has a big beak like a bucket. * Use 3+ descriptive strategies

Simply comparing two things such as "Some birds eat insects and some don't" is not enough to score well in description.

You will need to use a couple of different strategies – not just repeat the same type of description e.g. number

Example texts:

Standard text

Whales

Despite what many people think, whales are not fish. In fact they are mammals. Most whales live in the icy waters of the Arctic and Antarctic. There are two types of whales - toothed and baleen.

Odontocetes (toothed whales) use their teeth to grip their food rather than chew it. Toothed whales live in large groups, known as pods. Each pod usually contains one male with many females and their calves.

On the other hand, baleen whales do not have teeth. Instead they have whalebone that hangs down from their upper jaw. The whalebone strains out the food such as plankton and krill. Baleen whales feed during the summer and then migrate to warmer waters to breed.

continued over page

Coloured text is: Weaker level Standard level Stronger level

DESCRIPTION AND DETAILS (continued) — Scoring range 0–4

Stronger text

Whales

Whales come from the family known as cetaceans. Despite what many people think, they are not fish. In fact they are warm-blooded, air-breathing mammals. Most whales live in the icy waters of the Arctic and Antarctic and use their thick layers of fatty blubber to keep warm. There are two types of cetaceans - toothed and baleen.

Cetaceans such as dolphins are known as odontocetes and can have anywhere from 2-250 teeth. They use their teeth to grip their food such as squid and fish, rather than chew them. Their prey is located by using echolocation. The signals sent out from the front of their heads bounce off objects and return to the whale through their hollow lower jaw. Toothed whales live in large groups, known as pods. Each pod usually contains one male with many females and their calves.

Unlike their toothed relations, baleen whales such as humpback whales have two blowholes, not just one. They also live in smaller family-based groups and have only one mate. Instead of teeth, baleen whales have a series of plates, called whalebone that hang down from their upper jaw. They act like a sieve, straining out the food such as plankton and krill. Baleen whales feed during the summer and then migrate to warmer waters to breed.

Ways to develop your descriptions

Give an example

Some birds, like the penguin, cannot fly.

Give a reason

Oystercatcher birds have long legs so they can wade through shallow water.

Change a general statement

Even though most birds are wild animals, some can be kept as pets.

Give an explanation

Owls are carnivores, which means they eat meat.

Coloured text is: Weaker level Standard level Stronger level

VOCABULARY (the types of words used)		Scoring range 0–5
Weaker texts	**Standard texts**	**Stronger texts**
* Are very short texts * Contain very few content words * Use mostly modelled words from stimulus	* Use mostly simple words – food, lives, starts, called * Use some (around 3–5) precise words – diet, results, prey, machine, connected * May use content words from the stimulus material	* Consistently use many different precise words * Include writing that is fluent and articulate

Example texts:

Standard text

How lightning is formed

Lightning, is formed when electricity is released from storm clouds. A lightning strike can be several kilometres long.

Storm clouds form on warm days because moisture rises and cools. Positively charged bits rise to the top of the cloud. Negatively charged bits are heavier and move to the bottom of the cloud.

The positive and negative bits move towards each other. This movement creates a path of electricity called lightning.

For lightning to strike the ground there needs to be a gathering of positive charges on the ground. The negatively charged particles at the bottom of the cloud must jump to the positive charges on the ground. This is why it is important to seek shelter inside during a lightning storm.

Stronger text

Nature Strikes Back

Lightning, an unpredictable natural force, is caused by the discharge of electricity from storm clouds. It is released from these clouds as a giant elongated spark, and can be several kilometres long.

Storm clouds form on warm, humid days because evaporating moisture rises and cools. These tiny particles of water move around in air currents, collecting positive and negative charges.

Positively charged particles are light and therefore rise, which means that the top of the cloud becomes positively charged. Negatively charged particles are heavier and consequently move to the bottom of the cloud which therefore becomes negatively charged. As a result, a thundercloud is like a battery.

Positive and negative charges are attracted to each other. The effect of the negative charges jumping and joining the positive charges is to create a path of electricity. This discharge of electricity is called lightning.

Accordingly, for lightning to strike the ground there needs to be a gathering of positive charges on the ground below. The negatively charged particles at the bottom of the cloud must jump to the positive charges on the ground. This is why it is crucial to seek shelter inside during a lightning storm. Remaining outside can be very dangerous, especially if you are a positively charged particle!

Coloured text is: Weaker level Standard level Stronger level

COHESION
(and, but, so, because, after, before, while, during, since)

Scoring range 0–4

Weaker texts	Standard texts	Stronger texts
* Are short texts * Are missing cohesive links or have links which are wrong * Include most pronoun references that are correct * May use some simple synonyms e.g. big, large, huge	* Include most sentences that are linked correctly * Include all pronoun references that are correct * Use synonyms for topic words e.g. home, habitat, haven, dwelling, shelter	* Include all links that are correct * Allow the reader to easily follow the flow of ideas * Include a range of words and devices that are used to link sentences, ideas and paragraphs

Example texts:

Standard text

Exploring Mars

Mankind has always been fascinated by what lay beyond our own planet. In 1971 an orbiting spacecraft called Mariner 9 observed Mars and found that there were a number of canyons and channels.

Later two Viking spacecraft landed on Mars and took samples of soil. When they were analysed, the samples showed no evidence of life.

But NASA did not end the quest with that disappointment. They sent out the Mars Pathfinder and its small roving vehicle known as Sojourner, to continue the collection of information. However, Sojourner's mission was short lived because it had technical difficulties.

NASA sent out another mission known as the Mars Odyssey Orbiter. Then came two rovers, the Spirit and Opportunity. They found evidence of water on Mars.

NASA is still conducting missions to Mars. What will they find?

Stronger text

The search for life on Mars

The history of human exploration of Mars has been relatively short. Only recently has mankind taken up the challenge to explore the surface of the planet and try to find out if it has ever, or could ever, support life.

In 1971, an orbiting spacecraft called Mariner 9 observed Mars and found that there were a number of canyons and channels that appeared to have been carved out of the rocky landscape by floods and rivers.

Several years later, in 1976, two Viking spacecraft landed on Mars and took samples of soil. Unfortunately for scientists at the time, when they were analysed, the samples showed no evidence of life either then or in the past.

At the turn of the century, in 2001, NASA sent out another mission known as the Mars Odyssey Orbiter. They followed this up in 2004 with two rovers, the Spirit and Opportunity, which found evidence that water had once existed in Mars.

Recently, in July 2008, the NASA spacecraft Phoenix landed on the polar region of Mars. Its mission was to dig up samples of the frozen soil and to heat it up to see if there was water trapped in the soil. And there was! Now scientists have concrete evidence that water can be found on Mars.

It was a crucial discovery that has already led to further exploration of the Martian landscape with the 2012 Mars Rover mission. What will it find?

Coloured text is: Weaker level Standard level Stronger level

PARAGRAPHS

(how you group your ideas, arguments and details)

Scoring range 0–3

Weaker texts	Standard texts	Stronger texts
* Do not use paragraphs OR * Include one block of text OR * Random line breaks OR * A new line for each sentence	* Use paragraphs to separate introduction, body and conclusion * Include big sections of text * Have all paragraphs that focus on one idea * Have at least 1 paragraph that has a topic sentence and some supporting detail	* Have all paragraphs that include a topic sentence and some supporting detail * Are well organised and build up the text

Example texts:

Standard text

Seabirds are creatures which live close to the coast and spend a lot of their time out in the ocean, or in rock pools by the shore searching for food.

Wading birds, such as oystercatchers, live and feed along the shore. They have long spindly legs. They use their thin beaks to dig around for small animals in the mud. When they are out over the deeper ocean, birds need to be able to fly for a long time, so the albatross has very long wings so it can glide for hours and not use up too much energy. The penguin needs to move quickly through the water to escape from predators, so it has webbed feet and a torpedo shaped body. All seabirds nest on land. Some nest on cliffs, while others build nests from sticks, seaweed or even mud.

All seabirds have adapted to their environment in different ways.

Stronger text

Seabirds are creatures which live close to the coast and spend a lot of their time out in the ocean, or in rock pools by the shore searching for food.

Wading birds, such as oystercatchers, live and feed along the shore. They have long spindly legs to help them wade through shallow water. They use their thin beaks to dig around for small animals in the water and mud.

But not all seabirds look like this with long legs and beaks.

When they are out over the deeper ocean, birds need to be able to fly for a long time, so the albatross has very long wings so it can glide for hours and not use up too much energy. While the penguin needs to move quickly through the water to escape from predators, so it has webbed feet and a torpedo shaped body.

All seabirds nest on land. Some nest on cliffs to be safe, laying their eggs among rocks. While others build nests from sticks, seaweed or even mud. Some, like the penguin, make nests out of a flap of skin under their stomach.

Even though all seabirds have adapted to their environment in different ways, they all have one thing in common - their diet. Seabirds feed on a variety of sea life such as fish and small crustaceans. A flock of seabirds over the ocean can alert fishermen to large numbers of bait fish in the water.

WRITING

SENTENCE STRUCTURE

Scoring range 0–6

(this is all about the grammatical structure of a sentence – does it make sense?)

Weaker texts	Standard texts	Stronger texts
* Do not include complete sentences * Have very short texts * Include some simple sentences are correct	* Include mostly simple sentences that are correct and some compound sentences are correct * May have one or two complex sentences correct	* Have most sentences of all types are correct OR * All sentences are correct but there is little variety

If you make a mistake with your verb form or a preposition, it is counted as a sentence error.

At a score of 5/6 they may allow one small sentence error. A score of 6/6 means all are correct.

Examples:

Simple sentences	In 1872 there was a ship. It was called the Mary Celeste. It was drifting in the North Atlantic Ocean. There was no one on board. The crew had disappeared. The ten people on board were never seen again. The mystery remains today. What happened to the Mary Celeste?
Compound sentences	In 1872 there was a ship and it was called the Mary Celeste. It was found in the North Atlantic Ocean, but there was no one on board. There had been ten people on board, yet everyone had disappeared. Was there a terrible storm, or perhaps a giant octopus? The mystery remains today and may never be answered.
Complex sentences	In 1872, a ship called the Mary Celeste was found drifting in the North Atlantic Ocean - with no one on board. Some people thought that the ship had been attacked by a giant octopus, or that a whirlwind sucked the crew off the decks. But if these theories are correct, why were there no signs of damage on the ship? Ten people had set sail on the Mary Celeste: the captain, his wife and young daughter, and seven crewmen. They were never seen again - and the mystery of what happened to them has never been solved.

If you use a sentence using 'and' a lot, it will be an error.

To learn more about how to create complex sentences, refer to page 114 at the end of the writing section.

Coloured text is: Weaker level Standard level Stronger level

PUNCTUATION (full stop, capital letter, comma, speech marks, dash, brackets, apostrophe ...)		**Scoring range 0–5**
Weaker texts	**Standard texts**	**Stronger texts**
* Do not include evidence of punctuation OR * Include minimal punctuation such as capitals to start sentences and full stops to end sentences * Include stray capital letters to begin words which are not proper nouns, or in the middle of words	* Have almost all sentences with correct sentence punctuation and some examples of other correct punctuation (such as commas, apostrophe for contractions) * Do not have any stray capital letters * Include correct capitals for all proper nouns	* Include all sentence punctuation (capitals, full stops) that is correct * Include almost all examples of other punctuation that are correct (speech marks, dashes, brackets, commas, apostrophes)

Example texts:

Standard text

A bear and his tail

Do you know why brown bears have short tails? If you asked a scientist they would probably explain it in a scientific way.

The brown bear is found throughout the Northern Hemisphere. They live in mountain forests and open meadows. During winter they hibernate.

Brown bears are believed to have migrated to North America from Asia between 50 000 and 100 000 years ago. It was during this migration that the bears needed to adapt to their changing environment. Their tails became smaller and smaller until they look the way they do today.

However the explanation by the native Iroquois is quite different. It involves fox playing a trick on bear and getting him to stick his tail in an icy fishing hole until it froze over. When the bear tried to get up his long frozen tail snapped right off and left him with a short stumpy tail instead.

Stronger text

The Tale of a Bear

Do you know why brown bears have short tails? If you asked a scientist they would probably explain it like this:

The brown bear (ursus arcto) is found throughout the Northern Hemisphere, including North America and Canada. They live in mountain forests and open meadows. During winter they hibernate and aren't seen until early Spring.

Based on fossilised evidence, brown bears are believed to have migrated to North America from Asia between 50 000 and 100 000 years ago. It was during this migration that the bears needed to adapt to their changing environment. No longer did they need to have a long tail, so over several generations, their tails became smaller and smaller until they look the way they do today.

However the Iroquois tale of the brown bear's tail is quite different. It involves fox playing a trick on bear and getting him to stick his tail in an icy fishing hole until it froze over. When the bear tried to get up, his long frozen tail snapped right off and left him with a short stumpy tail instead.

Coloured text is: Weaker level Standard level Stronger level

SPELLING

Scoring range 0–6

Weaker texts	Standard texts	Stronger texts
* Do not include proper spelling (unless it is modelled words from the stimulus) OR * A few simple words correct (my, fun, must) OR * Less than 20 correct words written	* Include all simple words and almost all common words that are correct (again, their, wrong) * May have some difficult words correct (less than 10)	* Include all simple, all common, and some difficult (10+) words that are correct * May have a few challenging words correct

Guarantee, metamorphosis and organisation are examples of challenging words.

Habitat, predator, transformed, and collection are examples of difficult words with many syllables.

Example texts:

Standard text

How to make an electrical circuit

Before beginning the task, make sure you have all the materials you need (scissors, battery, electrical wire, light bulb, switch, alligator clips).

First of all, strip the plastic away from the ends of each piece of wire. Then attach each end of the wires to an alligator clip. After you have done this, clip one piece of electrical wire to the negative end of the battery and then take another piece of wire and attach it to the positive end of the battery. (The higher the voltag of the battery, the briter the light will be.)

Next, attach one of the free ends of electrical wire to the light bulb.

Now you need your final piece of electrical wire. Attach one end of it to the electrical switch and the other end to the light bulb. To complete the circuit, attach the last end of wire to the electrical switch.

Finally, to see if it works, flick the switch and you should see the light bulb light up. Click the switch again to break the circuit. This stops the flow of electricitee between the battery and the light bulb.

Stronger text

The construction of an electrical circuit

Before commencing the task, make sure you have all the appropriate materials needed to construct your electrical circuit (scissors, battery, electrical wire, an incandescent light bulb, switch, alligator clips). Being well prepared will almost guarantee a successful scientific experiment.

First of all, strip the plastic insulation away from the ends of each piece of wire. Then attach each end of the wires to an alligator clip. After you have done this, clip one piece of electrical wire to the negative end of the battery and then take another piece of wire and attach it to the positive end of the battery. (The higher the voltage of the battery, the brighter, or more luminous the light will be.)

Next, attach one of the free ends of electrical wire to the light bulb.

Now you need your final piece of electrical wire. Attach one end of it to the electrical switch and the other end to the light bulb. To complete the circuit, attach the last end of wire to the electrical switch. You have now successfully prepared an electrical circuit.

Finally, to see if it works, flick the switch and you should see the light bulb light up. Click the switch again to break the circuit. This discontinues the flow of electricity between the battery and the light bulb.

Coloured text is: Weaker level Standard level Stronger level

Planning an informative text

One effective way of planning your informative text, remembering you only have five minutes, is using a flow chart. Flow charts are excellent when writing explanations including life cycles or procedures such as directions and instructions because they help you to sequence the stages or steps clearly. Don't forget to try and think of some interesting and technical words to make your text cohesive and full of factual details.

Title
- From caterpillar to butterfly

1
- A female butterfly lays dozens of eggs on the leaves of plants.

2
- 3–7 days later these eggs will hatch and the young caterpillars will eat the leaves they were born on.

3
- The caterpillars will continue eating, almost non stop for the next 2–3 weeks as they grow.

4
- As they grow, the caterpillars will shed their exoskeleton several times and can dramatically change their appearance.

5
- When they shed their exoskeletons for the last time, the caterpillars will attach themselves to a branch or stem with silk and form their chrysalis around themsleves.

- 1–2 weeks later, the adult butterfly emerges from the chrysalis, dries out its wings and flies away to continue the life cycle.

Another good way to plan is to use a concept map. This helps you to think about the different aspects of the topic and organise some facts and details to support each area. Concept maps are useful when writing information and scientific reports.

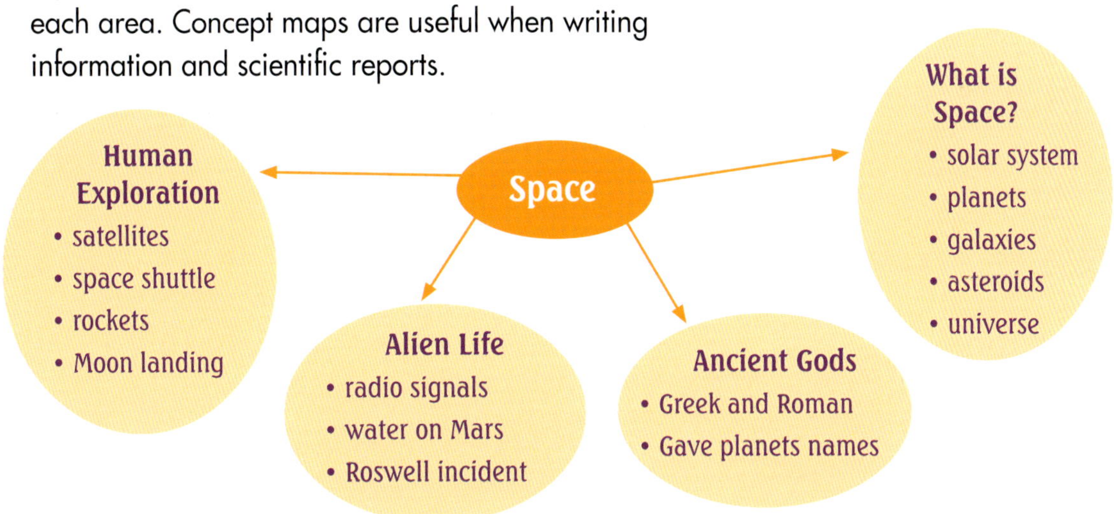

Vocabulary lists for informative writing

When you are trying to inform another person about a particular topic, you need to use special words. Often these words are factual or technical. Using these types of words will help your score in the vocabulary section of the marking criteria. If you learn how to spell the more difficult words, that will help you improve your spelling score as well. (See more about scores in the marking criteria section pages 91–102)

Ordinary word choice	Better word choices
make	build, construct, formulate, produce, assemble
home	habitat, shelter, safe haven
looks like	appearance, form
grow	develop, mature, produce
moves	slithers, creeps, scuttles
fly	soar, ascend, flutter
eat	gobble, consume, munch
turns into	changes, adapts, transforms
jump	bound, leap, spring, hurdle
find	locate, discover, uncover
look for	explore, search, investigate
first	original, initial, earliest
final	concluding, ultimate
has	includes, contains, features
stop	cease, discontinue, prevent
start	begin, launch, initiate
change	transform, alter, modify
give	provide, grant
bit	piece, component, element
send	transmit, propel, broadcast
break	damage, spoil, shatter
work	operate, function

Words to join/link ideas
and
so
if
since
after that
before
although
later on
because
for example
as well as
also
firstly
finally
but
as a result
to begin with
following
otherwise
despite
consequently
therefore

The informative writing begins

Once the five minutes planning time is up, you will have thirty minutes to write your text. Now that probably doesn't seem like a long time, so remember to concentrate on QUALITY and not just QUANTITY. However, you must remember to FINISH your text. A text without a conclusion may mean that you miss out on scoring some important marks.

A scaffold (outline) for an informative text (report genre)

Title: (something that identifies the topic and makes it sound interesting to the audience)
Introduction: This is a general opening statement. A few sentences (3–5) that classify the topic (put it into a group such as mammals, reptiles, space craft) and identify some examples.
Body: A series of paragraphs. Each paragraph will have a few sentences. The first sentence of each paragraph will be the topic sentence. Each paragraph will look at a different aspect of the topic e.g. appearance, habitat, diet or features, tools, uses. Each paragraph will give facts and details about the specific aspect of the topic to describe it.
Conclusion: A few sentences (2–4) that make a final statement about the topic, or give some interesting information that is not covered by one of the earlier paragraphs.

A scaffold (outline) for an informative text (explanation genre)

Title: (a how or why question)
Introduction: This is a general opening statement. A few sentences (3–5) that identify the topic. It looks at the significance of the topic being explained, when and why it occurs.
Body: A series of paragraphs. Each paragraph will have a few sentences. The first sentence of each paragraph will be the topic sentence. Each paragraph will look at a different stage or step in the process. Each paragraph needs to use connectives to sequence the events.
Conclusion: A few sentences (2–4) that make a final statement about the topic. What happens at the end of the process? Why is it important?

Getting a good start for an informative text

Informative texts need to make sure that they orientate the reader by giving important background information that answers:

- who
- where
- when
- why

Below are some different ways you can begin the opening statement of your information text.

Using the second person pronoun 'you' can help to include the reader.

Try this

Start with a **rhetorical question** (good for explanations) such as:

- Have you ever wondered what makes day and night?
- Why do clouds float when rain falls?
- When you think of codes, do you imagine a spy sending a message?

Use the topic 'the lifecycle of a frog' to write your own rhetorical questions to begin your text.

____

____

____

____

Try this

Use technical words in a topic statement.

Start with a **clear topic statement** (good for reports) such as:

- Formula one, also known as Grand Prix racing, is the fastest form of track racing in the world.
- The solid ground that we walk on is the Earth's crust, but below its surface, it is not at all like a piece of bread.
- The water cycle explains how water changes its form and moves between the Earth's oceans, atmosphere and land.

Use the topic 'transportation' (you may choose which form) to write your own clear topic statement to begin your text.

____

____

____

____

Start with **sentences that appeal directly to the audience** (good for reports and explanations) such as:

- Think of a volcano as a pimple on your face, the slightest pressure and it can explode!
- They mightn't look very pretty, but caterpillars are amongst the most amazing creatures in the world.
- No, the sky is not falling in, it's just a lunar eclipse!

Try this

Use the topic 'animals' (you can choose any type of animal) to write one or more sentences that appeal directly to your audience to begin your text.

____

____

____

____

Start with a **sentence that helps the audience understand the order of events** (good for explanations) such as:

- To understand how thunder occurs, first you need to know how lightning is created.
- Frogs are often seen as slimy and disgusting, but they are quite remarkable when you find out where they came from.
- Asteroids, yellow dwarfs and black holes; let's follow the astronomers as they discover what lies beyond our solar system.

You can also use these strategies and ideas to begin new paragraphs.

Try this

Use the topic 'reptiles' (as a report on different types of reptiles, or an explanation of their life cycle or how they hunt) to write a sentence to begin your text by explaining or hinting at the order of events.

____

____

____

____

The body of an informative text

When you are writing in an informative way, whether it is a report, explanation or procedure, it is important to remember that you are writing as an expert. This means that your writing should be FORMAL and not INFORMAL.

Formal writing creates a sense of confidence in the information being given. It shows that the writer wants their ideas to be taken thoughtfully.

Informal writing is more personal and relaxed, but it can also make the author appear not to be serious about the topic.

FORMAL WRITING
Unfortunately life as we know it is about to end. Over the past few months, astronomers have been tracking a gigantic asteroid known as *Youwannapieceofme.* As it approaches Earth, it is being influenced by the Sun's gravitational field and, as such, is on a collision course with the star that provides us with light, heat and of course – life! ✓

INFORMAL WRITING
Oh heck! We are all gonna die! Some astronomer dude has found this whopping great big rock somewhere out in space. He named it *Youwannapieceofme.* He reckons the Sun is pulling this thing closer and that soon they will smack into each other and – poof! No more Sun. That means we are done for too. No light, no heat, no me! I don't like the sound of that. Do you? ✗

Main ideas and supporting details

The main idea is also known as the topic sentence.

When writing informative texts, you need to make sure that each paragraph has a main idea along with some supporting evidence or details, usually in separate sentences within the paragraph.

Main idea → Your nose and ears are not a part of your skeleton.

Supporting details → They are actually made up of cartilage. Cartilage is more flexible than, but not as hard as, bone. Which is why you might break your arm, but it is really hard to break your ear! If you visit the museum, there is no use talking to the skeletons, because they cannot hear you.

Developing a paragraph

Within each paragraph you will need to include the following.

- A main idea (topic sentence)
- Facts and details (information)
- Words to join and link the ideas and events (connectives and conjunctions)
- Interesting words related to the topic (vocabulary)
- Accurate sentence markers (punctuation)

Here is an example:

Submarines are ocean-going vessels which are designed to be watertight so they can operate with stealth under water. It is sometimes said that they are the wolves of the sea.

Submarines look like a smooth caterpillar with a long rounded hull which is made up of two sections that have been welded together. The first section, the inner chamber, is designed to protect the submarine and those on board from the extreme pressures found deep in the ocean. The second section, the outer chamber, contains the ballast tanks, without which the submarines would be unable to submerge or rise up through the ocean depths.

Each ballast tank has small doors attached which open to allow the movement of water. The more water taken in to the ballast tanks, the deeper the submarine will submerge. In order to resurface, compressed air is forced into the ballast tanks. This expels the water back out into the ocean so the submarine can begin to rise.

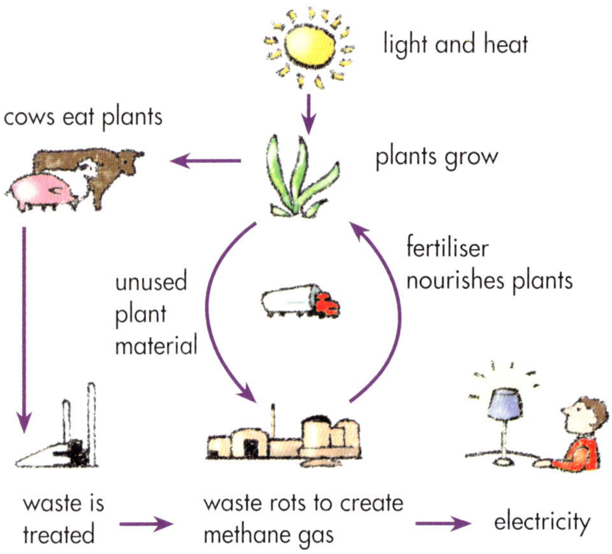

- Biogas is a naturally created gas from plants and animals.
- Animal manure (poo) is collected and mixed with waste plant material (not needed for food).
- As it rots, gas is created. This gas powers electrical generators.
- Some of the rotting material is also used for fertiliser.

Use the dot points to help create an interesting paragraph, using the pointers on the picture to assist you.

____

____

____

____

____

Concluding an informative text

The conclusion to an information text is usually quite short. It is used to present a final statement on the topic and to wrap up the information or to say what happens at the end or just after the process.

For example:

- The development of personal tablet devices has transformed the way in which people go about their daily lives.
- As you can see, sharks are very complex predators. It is little wonder that they are at the top of the food chain.
- The discovery of water on Mars was a crucial step that is certain to lead to further exploration into the future.

The final edit

Once your 30 minutes writing time is up, the teacher will tell you that you now have 5 minutes for editing. But if you haven't finished writing yet, don't worry; you can use some of the five minutes to complete your informative text.

Revising and editing your work is an important part of the writing process. This is where you have a chance to check your work for any silly errors and maybe even add something to improve it.

If you need to change something, don't waste time rubbing it out – just cross it out and write the new word above it.

Revision checklist:

- Do you have a good title that introduces the topic?
- Do you stay on the topic with all your ideas?
- Do you have a separate introduction that classifies or makes a general statement about the topic?
- Do all your sentences make sense?
- Have you used cohesive words and phrases to link your ideas between sentences?
- Have you used technical and interesting descriptive words throughout?
- Do you have each new aspect of the topic in a separate paragraph with some supporting details and examples?
- Do you have a conclusion to end the sequence of events or make a final statement on the topic?

Editing checklist

- If you missed any paragraph breaks, use this symbol [to show where the paragraph begins.
- Do all your sentences start with capital letters?
- Do all your sentences end with a full stop, exclamation mark or question mark?
- Do all proper nouns (names) begin with a capital letter?
- Have you accidentally put capital letters where they don't belong?
- Have you correctly used apostrophes for contractions? e.g. don't, can't, isn't
- Have you used commas when listing items?
- Have you spelt your words correctly?

Don't worry if you cannot spell a difficult word. Use it anyway because it will help you get a better score in the vocabulary section.

Try this

Use the following stimulus materials to help you plan, write and edit your own informative text. It would be a good idea to have a timer so that you can practise in a similar environment to the real NAPLAN test.

Today you will be writing a report.
This is also known as an information text.

The idea for your writing is

DINOSAURS

You need to think about:

- where they are found
- different types of dinosaurs
- what they looked like
- how they behaved
- what they ate

Remember to:

- plan your report before you begin
- write in sentences and paragraphs
- use interesting words and be careful with your spelling and punctuation
- check and edit your writing at the end

Try this

Today you will be writing an explanation.

You need to think about:

- the steps that happen in the process
- who is involved and what they do
- why different steps are important
- how it is made

Remember to:

- plan your explanation before you begin
- write in sentences and paragraphs
- use interesting words and be careful with your spelling and punctuation
- check and edit your writing at the end

HANDY HINTS FOR WRITING COMPLEX SENTENCES

A complex sentence is made up of a principal clause and one or more subordinate clauses. For example:

Check the depth of the pool (principal) before you dive in (subordinate).

The subordinate clause can begin with a conjunction:

- When the yeast has made the dough rise, it is ready to bake in the oven.
- If the egg is left unattended for too long, it will not hatch.
- Since the discovery of dinosaur skeletons, archaeologists have argued about why they became extinct.

A principal clause is the main clause in a sentence. It does make sense on its own, but gets more detail from the subordinate clause.

The subordinate clause can come anywhere in the sentence.

- When the mother penguins return to the rookery, they feed their chicks.
- The smallest dinosaur, as far as anyone knows, was the compsognathus.
- The mother seahorse lays the eggs, while the father incubates them in his pouch.

A subordinate clause depends on the principal clause for its meaning. It doesn't make sense on its own.

The subordinate clause can do the work of an adjective and describe a noun. In these sentences they always come after the noun they are describing.

- Steve Waugh was an Australian cricketer who was known for his old battered green cap.
- The burrow is found in the riverbank which is where the female will have her pups.

HANDY HINTS FOR PUNCTUATION

Punctuating sentences

Different types of sentences need different types of punctuation.

- Statement (tells the reader something) – uses a capital letter to start and a full stop at the end.
  Whales are the largest species of mammals.
- Question (asks something) – uses a capital letter to start and a question mark at the end.
  Why do volcanoes erupt?

- Exclamation (gives a feeling of surprise, anger or excitement) – uses a capital letter to start and an exclamation mark at the end.
  It is the most unusual phenomenon in nature!
- Command (tells someone what to do) – uses a capital letter to start and a full stop at the end.
  Give me the encyclopaedia.

Punctuating with commas

A comma is used to separate words or parts of sentences to help the reader understand the meaning.

- Commas in a list (to separate three or more items)
  There are many different types of stars such as white dwarfs, giants and supergiants.
- Commas in adverbial phrases and clauses
  The following day, the eggs begin to hatch.
- Commas to act as brackets (to contain extra information)
  Mercury, the closest planet to the Sun, is the smallest planet in our solar system.
- Commas to separate main clauses and dependent clauses in complex sentences
  Huddling together for warmth, the male penguins rely on each other for survival.
  Main (Principal) clause
  Dependent (subordinate) clause

Adverbial phrases and clauses give more details about how, when, where and why something is happening.

Punctuating with apostrophes

An apostrophe can be used to show missing letters in a contraction or the possession of an object by a person or character.

- Contractions
  it is = it's *they will = they'll*
  we are = we're *will not = won't*
- Possession (single owner)
  My dad's job *The bag's zipper*
  Jayden's pet ferret *Thomas' footy*
- Possession (plural owners)
  The wool of the goats = the goats' wool
  The feet of the caterpillars = the caterpillars' feet

In apostrophe of possession, if the person's name already ends with the letter 's', then the apostrophe goes after the 's'.

Advanced punctuation

- Dashes (–) are used to introduce a sudden surprise, to show an interruption of speech, or to add a final piece of information.
  Submarines travel silently – under water.
  "Your project will be due next Wednesday – no, make that Monday."
- Brackets ( ) are used to include extra information.
  The tyrannosaurus rex (tyrant lizard) once roamed that land we now call North America.
  My friend (a 12 year old geek) always has her head in a book.
  Most residents (4 out of 5) refused to sign the petition.
- Bullet points (•) are used for listing key points of information or ideas. They are found in reports and other informative texts.
  A good scientist:
  - *records their observations*
  - *deals with facts*
  - *never fudges the results.*

HANDY HINTS FOR PARAGRAPHING

A paragraph can be a single sentence, but it is usually made up of several sentences about a particular idea or topic. Paragraphs help readers follow a long story or text. They are shown by either indenting the first line, or by using a line break.

Paragraphs that are too long can be boring and lose the attention of the reader, while paragraphs that are too short seem jerky and not connected to the topic.

You need to start a new paragraph when:

- there is a new event *(After lunch, Later that day, When the milk has cooled)*
- there is a new time period *(The next day, Five hours later, The following afternoon)*
- the setting has changed *(Back at home, When the milk reaches the supermarket, Out in the meadow)*
- there is a new piece of information *(Another feature of the shark is, However not all birds)*
- a new character is speaking
- a new idea or argument is presented *(Another reason why, But not all cows, However it can be difficult when)*

LANGUAGE CONVENTIONS

When you sit for your Year 5 NAPLAN test, the language convention test is the first one you will do. It is made up of two sections:

1. Spelling (about 25 questions)
2. Grammar and punctuation (about 25 questions)

Always have a go even if you are not sure. You might just get it right!

SPELLING

The first section of the spelling test begins with the wrong word being identified and all you have to do is write the correct spelling.

The test will circle the word which is spelt incorrectly.

1. We made sandcastles at the (beech) on Sunday.

beach

There may also be a section where you are asked to label parts of an object in a picture like the following.

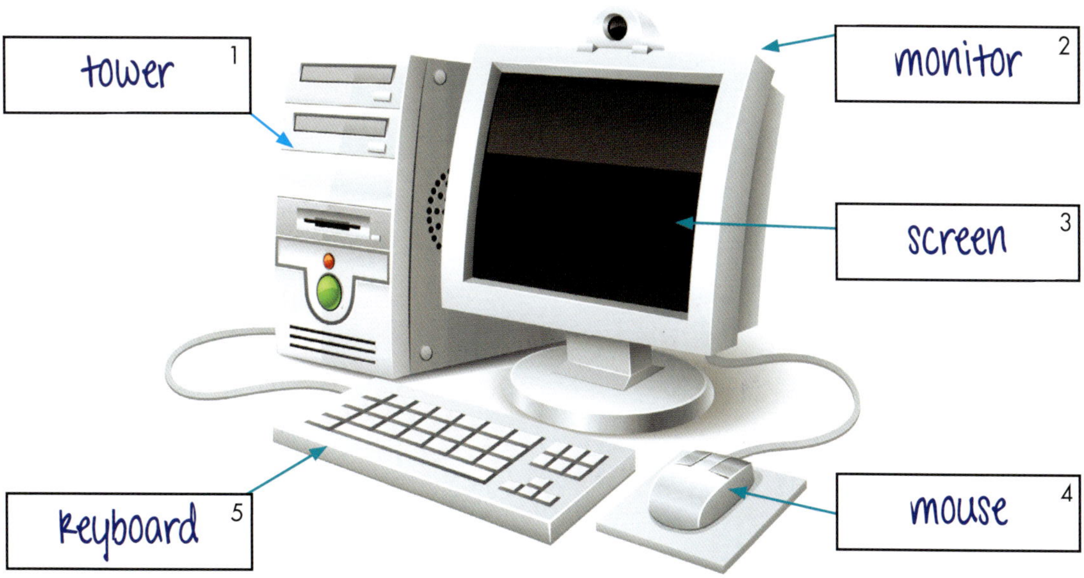

Some of the spelling questions may also include a little bit of reading. The test may give you a few short sentences that give information or tell a story.

The space shuttle

This is the space shuttle.

1. It travels so fast it breaks the (sownd) barrier. — sound
2. After lift-off, the (fule) pods drop off. — fuel
3. Once its mission is (compleat) the shuttle returns to earth. — complete

Sometimes looking at the wrong spelling can be confusing. So look at the sentence, remember it, say it, and then try to spell the word on your own.

Try this

The Mummy

Not all mummies give cuddles and look after you when you are sick.

Write the correct spelling

1. This mummy is an (ainchent) Egyptian Pharaoh (King). ______
2. When they died, the priests took their (bodee.) ______
3. The dead Pharaoh was (rapt) in bandages. ______
4. They were buried in large (piramids.) ______

The last part of the spelling test is the hardest. Here you are given short sentences with a word spelt incorrectly, but this time the test does not tell you which word is wrong. You have to work it out for yourself first, and then write the correct spelling in the box.

Try this

Write the correct spelling

1. Pineapples are a tropikal fruit grown in Queensland.
2. My teacher wears the most unushuall stripy socks.
3. Pedro once admited that he had picked his nose.
4. I am hopfull that I will pass my NAPLAN test.

Spelling rules to learn for NAPLAN

Eliminate the words you know are correct. Then look at common spelling rules that have been broken or spelling patterns that are wrong.

RULE 1:

The letter '**e**' at the end of a word usually makes the vowel in the word say its name.

For example:

shade tile dope rude

EXCEPTIONS

give come love were

Try this

Write the correct spelling

1. My favourite **reptisle** is the rattlesnake.
2. I am really good at swimming **backstroak**.
3. My bike was bent out of **shaip** when I crashed into the tree.
4. I had to **grop** around in the dark to find my torch.

RULE 2:

When two vowels go walking, the first one does the talking.

For example:

ai – says a as in bait
ea – says e as in read
ue – says u as in blue
oa – says o as in boat

EXCEPTIONS

oo such as boot, look **ou** such as shout, mouth, cough **oi** such as foil, coin

Try this

Write the correct spelling

1. I don't like lizards because they have **beedy** little eyes.
2. Doing all these NAPLAN tests hurts my **brane**.
3. I screamed so loudly at the footy that my **throte** hurt.
4. Which **venuu** are the Sydney Swans playing at?

RULE 3:

When the '**k**' sound follows a short vowel in a base word, it is spelt '**ck**'.

For example:

back neck kick sock truck

EXCEPTIONS

The exception is if another consonant follows the '**k**' sound (as in -**act**)
factor tractor doctor

Write the correct spelling

1. I play **fullbak** for my footy team.
2. Dad was relaxing in the **hammokk** on the beach.
3. We read a funny **limeric** about a leprechaun.
4. There was a **fleke** of mud on the carpet and boy was mum mad!

RULE 4:

When a syllable contains a SHORT vowel followed by ONE consonant, that consonant is doubled before adding an ending.

This rule is used for endings: ing ed er est y

For example: run – running hop – hopping skip – skipped
shop – shopped fun – funny big – biggest run – runner

Note: This rule also applies to short vowels at the beginning of a word – you double the consonant after it (as long as the short vowel is not part of a prefix (in, un, ex, en)).
For example: irrigate appointment announce opportunity

Write the correct spelling

1. Dad is not **admiting** to mum that he scratched the car.
2. Sam **plugd** the gap in the fence so Rover couldn't escape.
3. "I am going to **flatn** you!" my brother screamed.
4. "Give me your **atention**!" demanded the teacher.

RULE 5:

If a word ends with '**e**', drop the '**e**' before adding an ending that begins with a vowel or the letter '**y**'.
For example: ride – riding hope – hoped fame – famous shine – shiny

Keep the '**e**' before adding an ending that begins with a consonant.
For example: use – useful close – closely safe – safety price – priceless

Write the correct spelling

1. She stared in **amazment** at the Christmas lights.
2. Mum was **skakeing** in fear as the mouse crawled up her leg.
3. I put a **slimee** toad in my sister's lunchbox.
4. The look on my teacher's face when I handed in my homework was **prisless**.

RULE 6:

For a word that ends in '**y**', if the letter before the '**y**' is a consonant, change the '**y**' to '**i**' and add '**es**' or '**er**'.
For example: baby – babies cry – cries

For a word that ends in '**y**', if the letter before the '**y**' is a vowel, just add '**s**'.
For example: boy – boys play – plays monkey – monkeys

Try this

Write the correct spelling

1. The kindergarten children dressed up as **bunnys** for Easter.
2. Everyone knows Santa is too fat to come down **chimnees**.
3. Sari **enjoies** reading books about dragons.
4. The band was trying to play the **melodys**.

RULE 7:

For words ending in '**f**', if you hear the '**f**' sound in the noun plural, just add '**s**'
For example: roof – roofs reef – reefs

For words ending in '**f**', if you hear '**v**' in the noun plural, change the '**f**' to '**v**' and add '**es**'.
For example: shelf – shelves wolf – wolves

When changing a noun ending in '**f**' to a verb, you will need to change the '**f**' to '**v**' and add '**e**'.
For example: belief – believe proof – prove safe – save

Write the correct spelling

1. Why do **giraffs** have such a long neck?
2. Hamish always **strifes** to do his best.
3. Flood water **engulffes** everything in its path.
4. The tribal **chieves** had a meeting to discuss the issue.
5. We had to do it **ourselfs**.
6. The principal had to **relievf** the teacher on playground duty.

RULE 8:

Words that end in '**ch**', '**sh**' or '**x**', add '**es**' to make plural.

For example: fox – foxes church – churches bush – bushes

Write the correct spelling

1. The pimples left blemishs on her face.
2. Water really quenchz your thirst.
3. We had a boring lesson about prefixeez in spelling today.
4. The librarian is telling us about indexxs in factual texts.

Try this

RULE 9:

'**i**' before '**e**' except after '**c**'
In words where '**ie**' represents the long '**e**' sound, '**i**' is usually before the '**e**'
For example: piece siege field

However, the '**e**' is written before the '**i**' after the letter '**c**'
For example: receive ceiling conceit

EXCEPTIONS their weird species protein

Write the correct spelling

1. I had to retreave my soccer ball from the roof.
2. "What do you hope to acheev?" I asked myself.
3. Was it part of a decetful plan?
4. You need to have good personal hygine.
5. I do not perceve that as being a good idea.

RULE 10:

When '**all**' is used as a prefix, it only has one '**l**'

For example: alright also

Write the correct spelling

Try this

1. Has the game started allready?
2. It was fun, allthough I won't do it again.
3. "But you allways get what you want!"
4. Thank goodness school is orllmost over.

RULE 11:

When the '**ch**' sound follows a short vowel, it is spelt '**tch**'.

For example: match witch clutch

EXCEPTIONS much rich which

Write the correct spelling

1. I am going to switz lunches with my sister.
2. Let's play fech with Rover.
3. There was a computer glitzh and I lost all my work.
4. The rose thorns scrached my arm.

RULE 12:

The letter combinations '**ai**', '**ui**' or '**oa**' are never used at the end of a word.

RULE 13:

The letter 'q' is always followed by the letter 'u', EXCEPT when it is used in acronyms such as QANTAS.

Other spelling tips

Silent letters

- At the beginning of the word e.g. **w**rite
- At the end of a word e.g. lam**b**
- In the middle of a word e.g. s**w**ord

Write the correct spelling

1. I borrowed too much money and now I am in **det**. [ ]
2. The umpire blew his **wissle** to signal the end of the match. [ ]

Sometimes there is no rule for how to spell a word correctly. A good way to check is to write it different ways and see which one looks best.

Try this

AR or ER word endings

Write the correct spelling

1. The **caterpillher** was munching on the leaves. [ ]
2. Police in the **helicopta** swooped down for a good look. [ ]

EE or EA words

Write the correct spelling

1. The splinter was removed with a pair of **twezers**. [ ]
2. The price of petrol is going to **increse**. [ ]

ION words

Write the correct spelling

1. "The **decison** is up to you," said my teacher. [ ]
2. I will never understand long **divishon**! [ ]

GH words (augh/ough)

Try this

1. "That is **enuf**!" I yelled.
2. If only I had **cort** the ball, we could have won the game.
3. This is a major **breakthrew** according to the politicians.
4. The man's **dorta** waved him goodbye from the school gate.

Write the correct spelling

OUS words

1. Motor sports can be very **dangerus**.
2. I love to be **adventurus** in the great outdoors.

Write the correct spelling

Commonly used words

Circle the correct spelling of each word.

1. Sound out the words
2. Break them into syllables or segments
3. Which one looks right?

choise	chois	choic	choice
wile	whyl	while	whisle
unusul	unusual	unuseual	unushual
uncul	unkle	uncle	uncal
ocean	oshean	oshen	ocen
bicicle	bycycle	bicycle	bisycle
wuld	woold	woud	would
sudenly	suddnle	suddenly	suddenle
weather	wethar	weathar	wethere
favorit	favourite	favouright	faveorite

Try this

GRAMMAR

The second part of the language conventions test looks at Grammar and Punctuation.

In the grammar questions, you may be asked to:

- **choose which word best fits in a sentence**

Which word correctly completes the sentence?

Have you found _________ bag yet?

- ○ you
- ● your
- ○ yours
- ○ you're

Read the sentence using each word. Which way sounds the best?

- **choose words which have a special function (job) in the sentence**

Which word takes the place of a naming word in the sentence?

Percy likes eating apples because they are sweet and crunchy.

- ○ apples
- ○ Percy
- ● they
- ○ crunchy

The question says 'takes the place of', so you can ignore all the real naming words (Percy, apples). Look for a word used instead of one of these nouns.

- **choose words which are not needed in a sentence**

Which word is NOT needed in this sentence?

The busy shoppers ascended up the escalator to the next level.

- ○ busy
- ○ ascended
- ● up
- ○ next

Read the sentence four times, each time leaving out one of the words. Which way sounds best?

- **choose the sentence which matches a particular purpose**

Which sentence is a statement?

- ○ Go away!
- ● My favourite football team is the Bulldogs.
- ○ Can it be my turn next?
- ○ What will happen in the next episode?

A statement gives facts or expresses an idea.

- **choose what a word means in a sentence, or what it relates to**

Read the sentence again, each time replace the word 'their' with one of the answer choices. Which one sounds right?

In the sentence, what does the word **their** refer to?

The teachers were in the staffroom talking about their classes.

○ the talking ○ the classes
○ the staffroom ● the teachers

- **identify which sentence is correct or incorrect**

These types of questions are more difficult, because you have to look at grammar (word forms and word order) and punctuation.

Which sentence is correct?

○ Frank and me are the best at hip hop dancing.
○ Frank and myself are the best at hip hop dancing.
● Frank and I are the best at hip hop dancing.
○ Frank and mine are the best at hip hop dancing.

- **identify the word which has a particular purpose in a sentence**

Find the nouns (naming words) first. Then see which one uses a capital letter (names of places are often proper nouns). Don't be tricked by the first word of the sentence beginning with a capital letter.

Which word is the name of a place?

Ocean view apartments are popular in the city of Cairns.

○ Ocean ○ apartments
● Cairns ○ city

- **choose two correct answers**

In these types of questions, they will often put one correct answer with one wrong answer to try to trick the people who do not read the question carefully. Always check BOTH answers and not just the first one.

The answers will be in the same order as the gaps in the sentence.

Which words correctly complete the sentence?

Yesterday I went shopping ______ bought a present ______ you.

● and for
○ and to
○ when with
○ where for

- **identify which word or words could replace other word/s in a sentence**

Which word or words could be replaced with **we've**?

○ weave
● we have
○ we will have
○ we would have

In a contraction (shortened form of two words), the apostrophe replaces one or more letters.

- **identify sentences which are incorrect, or where a word or words have been used incorrectly**

In which sentence is the word **of** used incorrectly?

○ He seems very sure of himself.
○ Most of our class forgot to do their homework this week.
○ Yesterday I had a slice of watermelon for lunch.
● I wish I could of gone fishing with dad.

- **identify the replacement for a word**

Which word could be used to replace **ma'am** in the following sentence?

"Can I help you with your bags ma'am?" asked the taxi driver.

○ Mad mum
● Madam
○ Mad man
○ Mad I am

- **identify the correct tense to be used in a sentence**

Which words correctly complete the sentence?

We __________ to see the V8 race at Bathurst next year.

○ were going
○ have gone
● are going
○ have went

Even though you want to get the test finished quickly, take the time to check each possible answer. That way you can eliminate silly errors and help you to get the best score you can.

- **make connections between some sentences and information supplied (such as in a diagram, chart or table)**

Which sentence best conveys the information from the chart?

Animal	Type	Habitat	Diet
Snake	Reptile	Hollow logs	Small mammals
Frog	Amphibian	Ponds	Insects
Crocodile	Reptile	Rivers	Fish, dogs, cows, sheep

- ○ Snakes and crocodiles are reptiles and frogs are amphibians and they all eat insects.
- ○ Amphibians live in ponds and reptiles live in hollow logs but small mammals are the diet of snakes and large mammals are the diet of crocodiles.
- ● Both snakes and crocodiles are reptiles and eat mammals, while frogs are amphibians and eat insects.
- ○ While frogs live in ponds, and snakes live in hollow logs, because crocodiles live in rivers and eat larger animals.

- **identify which word or words cannot be used for a particular purpose**

Which of these words cannot be used as a singular noun (only one)?

- ○ camera
- ○ child
- ● people
- ○ keyboard

- **use the structure of the sentence to work out the order of events**

What happened first?

Before we went fishing, mum made us tidy our rooms and then brush our teeth.

- ○ They brushed their teeth.
- ○ They went fishing.
- ○ They left the house.
- ● They cleaned their rooms.

Which word best completes the sentence?

There are far too _______ tests at school!

- ◯ much
- ◯ many
- ◯ more
- ◯ most

If the items can be counted, then use 'many'. e.g. One cat, two cats. If it can't be counted, then use much.

Which word best completes the sentence?

"Mum, can I go to _______ house after school?"

- ◯ hers
- ◯ him
- ◯ his
- ◯ them

If someone owns the item 'the house', then use a possessive pronoun (their, his, her).

Try this

Which words best complete the sentence?

_______ NAPLAN is over, I will be happy _______ I have to do it again in year 7.

- ◯ Once until
- ◯ When so
- ◯ While and
- ◯ Because as

Remember to read the sentences using each of the different possible answers.

Which word or words are not needed in the sentence?

Today was the worst most horrible day of my life!

- ◯ Today
- ◯ most horrible
- ◯ of my
- ◯ worst

Things to know about NAPLAN grammar questions

They will use questions or types of grammar that students commonly have problems with such as:

Homophones (For example: to, two, too)

Homophones are words that sound the same but have different spelling and meaning.

Which word best completes the sentence?

That's not fair! ______ going to the movies without me!

◯ Their ◯ There ◯ They're ◯ Thair

When you get stuck, take a deep breath and ______ to think about it.

◯ pores ◯ paws ◯ pours ◯ pause

Verb forms (For example: ran, run, running)

Sometimes verbs change their form for different tenses (past, present or future). These are called irregular verbs.

Which word best completes the sentence?

Last night my friend ______ to my house for a sleepover.

◯ come ◯ came ◯ comed ◯ coming

We ______ on an excursion to the museum tomorrow.

◯ go ◯ goed ◯ going ◯ are going

Subject / verb agreement

Plural subjects need to have plural verb forms (we are here). Single subjects need single verb forms (I am here).

Which word best completes the sentence?

Sally Pearson ______ over hurdles like a gazelle.

◯ jump ◯ jumping
◯ jumpers ◯ jumps

The waves ______ against the shoreline.

◯ pound ◯ pounds
◯ are pound ◯ pounding

Try this

Pronoun referencing (For example: *Ben* sat down. *He* was tired)

Pronouns take the place of a noun.

Which word best completes the sentence?

The builders were upset because it was too wet for ______ to work.

◯ it ◯ them ◯ him ◯ his

Pronoun referencing (For example: *Ben* sat down. *He* was tired)

Which words best complete the sentence?

Sarah asked Elisha, "Can ______ have some of ______ chips please?"

- ◯ you my
- ◯ I you
- ◯ me yours
- ◯ I your

Prepositions (For example: on, in, down, onto, against)

Which word best completes the sentence?

Sometimes I like to go to the beach ______ myself and watch the surfers getting dumped.

◯ with ◯ by ◯ between ◯ from

Mum and dad are pleased ______ my results in NAPLAN.

◯ sat ◯ for ◯ with ◯ to

A preposition is a word that gives the position of an object.

Articles (a, an, the)

Which word best fits the sentence?

I saw ______ great pair of soccer boots on sale yesterday.

◯ this ◯ a ◯ these ◯ the

The snake is ______ animal that I will always detest.

◯ a ◯ that ◯ the ◯ an

Try this

Conjunctions (For example: and, so because, if)

Which word best completes the sentence?

It was cold and windy ______ we still wanted to play outside.

◯ if ◯ but ◯ while ◯ soon

Which words best complete the sentence?

The culprit was ______ the dog ______ the cat. It was the goldfish!

- ◯ either or
- ◯ so and
- ◯ neither nor
- ◯ finally but

Which word best completes the sentence?

______ the time mum arrived, water balloons were scattered everywhere!

◯ When ◯ By ◯ Finally ◯ Suddenly

Conjunctions are words that join ideas together in a sentence.

Some important grammatical vocabulary

Proper nouns	Names of people and places	Sydney, Mr Symonds, Derrick, Mt Fuji
Common nouns	Names of things	chair, face, computer, ball, team, boys
Pronouns	Words that replace a noun	I, me, my, they, us, our, she, them, you
Verbs	Words that gives action, speech or thoughts	run, jump, said, mumble, believe, think
Adverbs	Words that describe a verb	slowly, carefully, yesterday, quickly
Adjectives	Words that describe a noun	red, two, crumpled, messy, dirty, fun
Prepositions	Words that identify the position of an object	in, on, under, between, in front, behind
Conjunctions	Words that combine ideas in a sentence	and, but, so, because, if, although, yet
Articles	Words used before a noun or noun group	a, an, the

Try this

More tips and tricks for common grammar errors

The preposition 'between' is used for two things, 'among' is used for three or more things.

We divided the lollies ______ the eight of us in the group.

- ◯ beside
- ◯ among
- ◯ between
- ◯ with

Not all verbs change when using different tense.

Yesterday I ______ the ball over the fence.

- ◯ hitted
- ◯ hitting
- ◯ hit
- ◯ hits

Some words take irregular forms.

I would like to know how that was ______.

- ◯ do
- ◯ done
- ◯ did
- ◯ dided

Verbs can be contracted. This is a common error. could've = could have

Hey, you ______ done that!

- ◯ must-a
- ◯ must and
- ◯ must of
- ◯ must have

PUNCTUATION

Punctuation questions are mixed up with grammar questions in the Language Conventions test. You can see what that looks like in the practice test section on page 133.

Before you complete your NAPLAN tests, it is a good idea to understand the following types of punctuation.

1. Sentence punctuation

- Statements (start with a capital letter and end with a full stop) usually give some information.

My favourite sport is cricket.

- Questions (begin with a capital letter and end with a question mark) ask for some information or an answer.

Where are we going on our excursion?

- Exclamations (begin with a capital letter and end with an exclamation mark) are used to show shock, surprise or anger.

I can't stand it when the Bulldogs lose!

If the question is part of direct speech, then the question mark goes inside the speech marks – like this:
"Why did you poke your sister?" Mum asked.
Mum asked, "Why did you poke your sister?"

If the exclamation is part of direct speech, then the exclamation mark goes inside the speech marks – like this:
"I can't stand it when the Bulldogs lose!" her sister yelled.
Her sister yelled, "I can't stand it when the Bulldogs lose!"

2. Capitalisation

As you have seen, all sentences, no matter what their purpose, must begin with a capital letter. But there are other ways in which capital letters are used.

- For the beginning of direct speech

Looking at the dragon, Timon said, "You shouldn't smoke because it is bad for your health."

- For the first letter of a proper noun

This year we will celebrate Christmas with Evan and his family.

Proper nouns are names of important people, places, events and things.

- For the personal pronoun 'I', including contractions using 'I'

I wouldn't go in there right now because I've taken off my shoes.

3. Apostrophe for contractions

Be careful with the contraction it's. It means it is. You do not use an apostrophe when the word its is used to mean ownership. E.g. The elephant flapped its ears.

Contractions are made when two words are joined together and one or more letters are removed and replaced with an apostrophe. The words still have the same meaning.

I can't (cannot) stand it when my little sister sings.

I'm (I am) finished but you will have to try again.

My teacher said she's (she is) going crazy and I don't (do not) blame her.

4. Apostrophe for possession

Possessive pronouns such as its, yours, hers, his, DO NOT need an apostrophe to show possession.

Possession means ownership. To show ownership with nouns, the apostrophe says 'of' or 'belongs to'. For example: the dog's tail = the tail belonging to the dog.

Here is Blake's NAPLAN guide.

The sign on the car said Mum's taxi.

The baby's rattle was covered in dribble.

If there is more than one (plural) owner, then the apostrophe is placed after the 's'.

The cats' whiskers (the whiskers of the cats)

The boys' filthy soccer shorts (the shorts belonging to all the boys)

The teachers' grey hairs (the grey hairs belonging to the teachers)

5. Commas

Commas are used in different ways.

- To separate items in a list.

Always use the word 'and' before the last item in a list.

Last night I did some homework, watched TV and then went to bed.

- To separate clauses in a sentence.

If you forget to do your homework, say the dog ate it.

- To act as brackets to contain extra information.

Susan, my next door neighbour, likes to sing Justin Bieber songs.

- To separate direct speech from the rest of the text.

"We are going to lose tomorrow," Derrick moaned.

Derrick moaned, "We are going to lose tomorrow."

6. Speech marks

These are used to show the actual words spoken by a person or character.

"The dog ate my homework," Mitch said.

"The dog ate my homework!" Mitch shouted.

Mitch said, "The dog ate my homework."

Mitch shouted, "The dog ate my homework!"

"It wasn't my fault," Mitch said, "because the dog ate my homework."

The punctuation for the spoken sentence goes inside the speech marks.

If the spoken sentence ends with an exclamation mark or a question mark, you don't need to use a comma as well. For example:
"Can I come?" asked Maria.

7. Brackets

These are used to include extra information.

The car (with a top speed of 145 km/h) crashed into the barrier.

Captain James Cook (1728-1779) sailed on the ship, Endeavour.

8. Dashes

These are used to introduce a sudden surprise or dramatic ending, or to show an interruption in speech.

The children dragged themselves home - soaking wet but safe.

"And as the runners round the bend, Slippery Samuel - no Bellyfull Barry is in the lead!"

Sometimes there are questions in the NAPLAN reading test involving these types of punctuation, their purpose and their uses.

In this section of the NAPLAN test, the questions may appear differently. There will still be questions like this:

Which of the following sentences has the correct punctuation?

- Dogs make the best pets.
- dogs make the best pets.
- Dogs Make The Best Pets.
- dogs make the best pets?

But there may be other questions like this:

Shade one bubble

Shade ONE bubble to show where the missing comma should go.

I was testing hard boiled soft boiled and raw eggs to see which ones bounced the best.

Or this:

Which words and punctuation correctly complete the sentence?

When shall we ________ says it will be soon.

- start mum
- start. Mum
- start? Mum
- Start. Mum

You need to use a capital letter to begin the sentence.

Make sure you check every word and every piece of punctuation in each sentence – just in case there is a stray capital letter or missing full stop. The little things do count!

LANGUAGE CONVENTIONS PRACTICE TEST

Over the next few pages, there are several sample questions to help you prepare for NAPLAN. There are a range of different types of questions. If you get stuck, check out some of the previous activities and tips to help you.

In the sentences below, the spelling mistakes have been circled. Write the correct spelling for each circled word in the box.

1. Looking at my refleshon in the mirror is scary when I have bed hair!
2. Is that an alien spaceship in the distanss?
3. The dirty clothes in the lorndry smelt terrible.
4. The monster's hypnotic eyes bewichd its victim.
5. "If only I was more athleteak," moaned Jeremiah.
6. Please put the contayener on the bench.
7. In NAPLAN, if you are not sure of the answer, you can still have a gesse.

Look at the picture. The text is about this picture. Each line of the text has ONE spelling mistake. Write the correct spelling of the word in the box at the end of the line.

8. There is a problem with the car's enjin.
9. The mehcanik is trying to fix the broken part.
10. Hoapfuly it will be running again soon.
11. I need it repared for my weekend away in the mountains.

Each sentence has ONE word that is spelt incorrectly.
Write the correct spelling of the word in the box at the end of the line.

12. Doctors help prevent diseezes that make people sick. [ ]

13. Bewhere of the grumbling bunyip in the billabong. [ ]

14. My passport signachure looks like spider scrawl. [ ]

15. Sometimes I wish my teacher would dissapear into thin air. [ ]

16. "I like to live dangerusle," the injured stunt man replied. [ ]

17. **Which word/s correctly completes the sentence?**

The teacher [ ] her class a frightening vampire story every day.

◯ telling ◯ tells ◯ tell ◯ was telling

18. **What does 'them' refer to?**

Dijon and Mustard are Mr and Mrs Hot's family pets. They often play with them in their backyard.

◯ Mr and Mrs Hot ◯ they
◯ the family ◯ Dijon and Mustard

19. **Shade two bubbles to show where the missing speech marks should go.**

◯ Before they left, ◯ Julia asked, ◯ How are we going to get home ◯ ? ◯

20. **Which of the following sentences is correct?**

◯ Samuel was preparing to play a trick on the Principal.
◯ Samuel were preparing to play a trick on the Principal.
◯ Samuel was preparing to playing a trick on the Principal
◯ Samuel is preparing to playing a trick on the Principal.

21. **Which sentence has the correct punctuation?**

- ◯ until principal wreck returns from the mental institution the children are in control
- ◯ Until principal wreck returns from the mental institution, the children are in control.
- ◯ Until Principal wreck returns, from the mental institution, the children, are in control.
- ◯ Until Principal Wreck returns from the mental institution, the children are in control.

22. **Which of the following correctly completes the sentence?**

The teacher asked that the injured girl be ☐ to as soon as possible.

◯ sees ◯ seen ◯ see ◯ seeing

23. **Which word in the sentences is a preposition?**

Look out! Don't wave the stick in the air.

◯ in ◯ out ◯ look ◯ don't

24. **Which words in the sentence need brackets?**

Astrologists people who study space recently reclassified Pluto as a dwarf planet.

- ◯ Astrologists
- ◯ Study space recently
- ◯ a dwarf planet
- ◯ people who study space

25. **Shade one bubble to show where the missing apostrophe should not go.**

Today, Josh◯s family wanted to go to the mountain◯s but they can◯t because it◯s snowing.

26. **Which of the following sentences is correct?**

- ◯ How on earth am I going to do that I asked?
- ◯ How on earth am I going to do that? I asked.
- ◯ "How on earth am I going to do that I asked?"
- ◯ "How on earth am I going to do that?" I asked.

END OF TEST

NUMERACY

Time flies, so don't waste time

The numeracy test has 40 questions.

You will have 50 minutes to answer those questions. That means you will have more than a minute for each question. This should be plenty of time so there is no need to rush.

It is a good idea to practise doing that number of questions in the time. *(There is a practice paper at the end of the numeracy section of this book.)*

Read the questions carefully. Make sure you answer the question that has been asked. For example, if the question asks how many are left, make sure your answer is the number left not those taken away.

In the numeracy test the questions might be multiple-choice, where you will need to colour in a circle, or short answer, where you will need to write the answer (usually a number).

Make sure that you answer every question. For multiple-choice questions, make sure that you have coloured in a circle for every question, and only one circle.

Take time to think whether your answer makes sense. If a girl has only \$3 and spends \$2·50, she can't have \$2 left.

The numeracy part of this book is divided into three sections.

There are different ways to try to find the answers to questions. Section 1 gives you some examples of some of those different ways.

Section 2 is a checklist of the things that you should know.

Section 3 is a practice paper.

Finally, there are answers to all of the questions that you should try.

WORK IT OUT!

Some questions will be quite straightforward. You will just need to work out the answer like you do at school every day!

When you know the answer, either write it in the box or colour in the circle next to that answer if it is a multiple-choice question.

David spins the arrow on this spinner.
On what number is it most likely to stop?

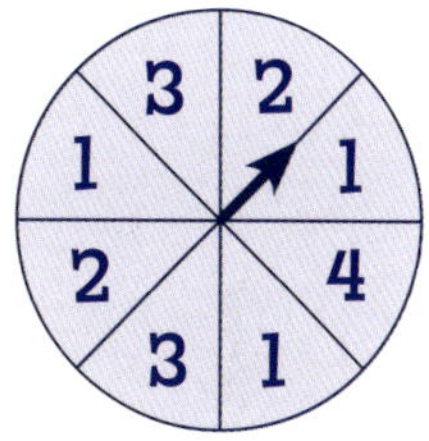

1 (filled) 2 3 4

Explanation:
The spinner is equally likely to stop on any of the sectors. More sectors have 1 than any other number. So, the spinner is more likely to stop on 1.

38 + 16 =

42 44 52 54

What do you need to add to 38 to make 40?

Try this

Wayne drew some shapes.

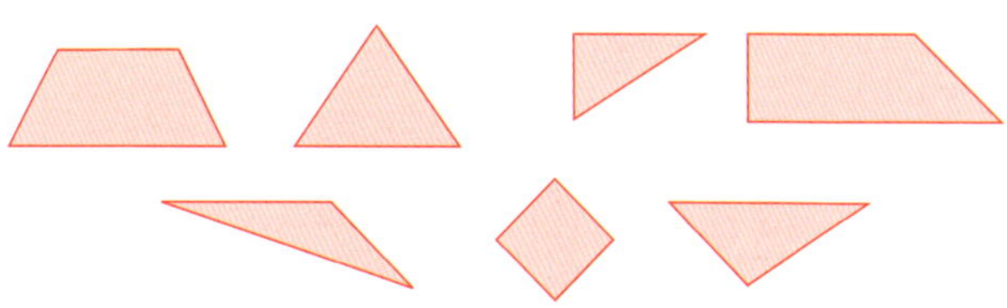

How many triangles did Wayne draw? ☐

How many of the shapes have exactly 3 sides?

Norah left home at 9:30 am. She was out for $1\frac{1}{2}$ hours.
At what time did Norah get home again?

10:30 am 10:45 am 11:00 am 11:15 am

What time will it be half an hour after 9:30? What time will it be another hour after that?

CHECK IT OUT!

Sometimes in multiple-choice questions you have to look at the choices to decide which one is correct. The question does not make sense on its own. The answers are part of the question.

Which has $\frac{1}{3}$ shaded?

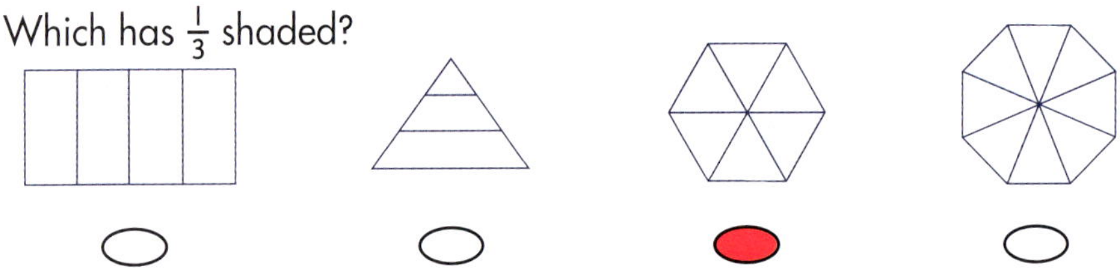

Explanation: $\frac{1}{3}$ means one of three **equal** parts.

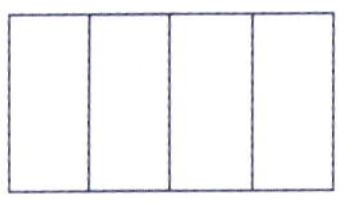

This has one of four equal parts shaded. It is $\frac{1}{4}$.

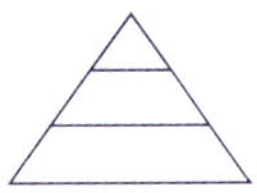

This has one of three parts shaded but they are not equal parts.

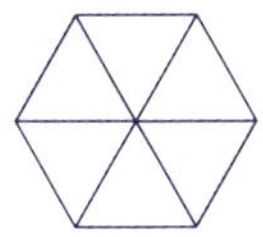

This has two of six equal parts shaded. Now two out of six is the same as 1 out of 3. It is $\frac{1}{3}$.

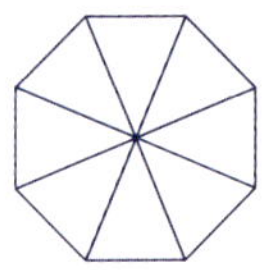

This has three of eight equal parts shaded. It is $\frac{3}{8}$.

Try this

Try to picture something as long as each of the measurements in the choices.

This is a picture of a car. Which of these is closest to the length of a real car?

1 metre 4 metres 14 metres 41 metres

One option is obviously too big and one option is obviously too small.

Which of these has the same value as 6 × 8?

12 × 16 3 × 4 7 × 7 12 × 4?

Try this

TRY IT OUT!

In multiple-choice questions, one of the given choices must be the correct answer. Although there might be other ways to work out the answer, sometimes it is easier to look at the choices to find the one that works.

Helen has 47 pencils. Lara has 33 pencils. How many pencils should Helen give to Lara so they both have the same number?

80	40	14	7
○	○	○	●

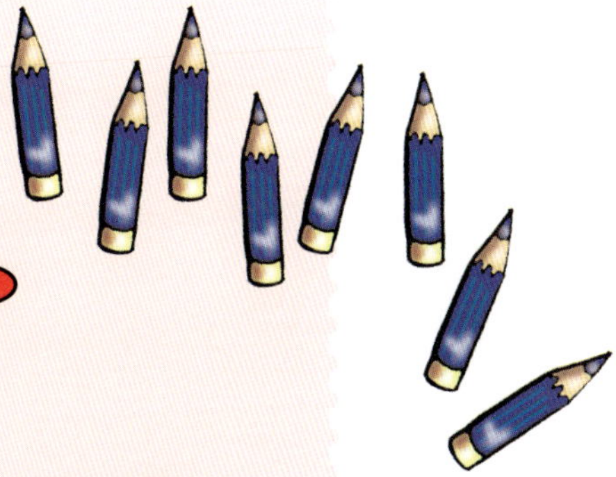

Explanation:

Try each of the choices.

80: Helen does not have 80 pencils, so she cannot give 80 to Lara. This is not the answer.

40: If Helen gave 40 pencils to Lara she would only have 7 left. Lara would have 73 pencils. This is not the answer.

14: Now 47 – 14 = 33 so if Helen gave 14 pencils to Lara she would have 33 left. 33 + 14 = 47 so Lara would have 47 pencils. This is not the answer.

7: Now 47 – 7 = 40 so Helen would have 40 pencils left. 33 + 7 = 40 so Lara would now have 40 pencils. Helen and Lara both have the same number of pencils, so this is the answer.

John's team is playing in the basketball competition. The team has played 6 games and has not had any losses. They have 8 points altogether.

How many games has John's team won?

2	3	4	5
○	○	○	○

BASKETBALL COMPETITION	
Win	2 points
Draw	1 point
Loss	0 points

Because there were no losses, the number of wins plus the number of draws must be 6.

Rufus starts with an odd number.
He adds 7 and then halves his answer.
Then he subtracts 2 and after doing that his answer is 4.

What number did Rufus start with?

1	3	5	7
○	○	○	○

Begin with the number in each choice and follow the steps that Rufus took. Only one choice would give Rufus an answer of 4.

DON'T BE FOOLED!

Although the examiner is probably not actually trying to trick you, the answers that you would get if you make the most common mistakes will be some of the choices in a multiple-choice question.

Don't rush! You must read the questions carefully.

Watch out for words like 'not', 'more' and 'least'.

Alexander wants to build a fence around this paddock.

How many metres long will the fence be?

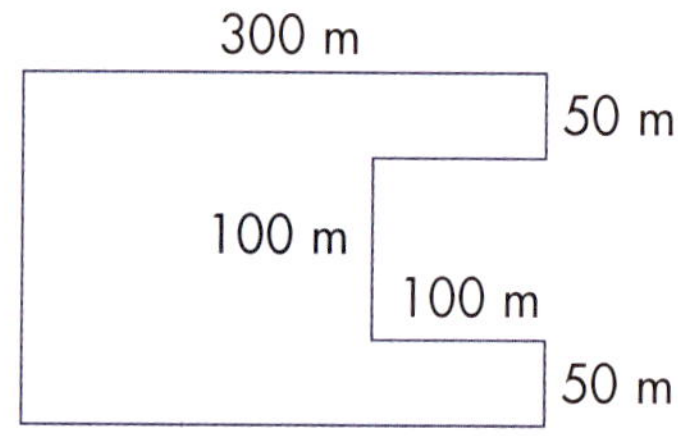

600 ○ 800 ○ 1000 ○ 1200 ●

Explanation:

Not all the measurements are shown so you can't just add the ones you see. Because the top is 300 m long the bottom must also be 300 m long. The right hand side is 50 m + 100 m + 50 m or 200 m so the left side must also be 200 m. Finally, because the measurement at the bottom of the gap is 100 m the measurement at the top would also be 100 m.

Now 300 + 300 + 200 + 200 + 100 + 100 = 1200.
So the length of the fence is 1200 metres.

Note: The question was asking for the perimeter of the paddock.

Try this

The two maps are facing different directions.

Ruby is going to stay at the holiday camp. She has a map, which shows the camp on Jackson Road. Ruby also has a plan of the camp.

Which of these is closest to Jackson Road?

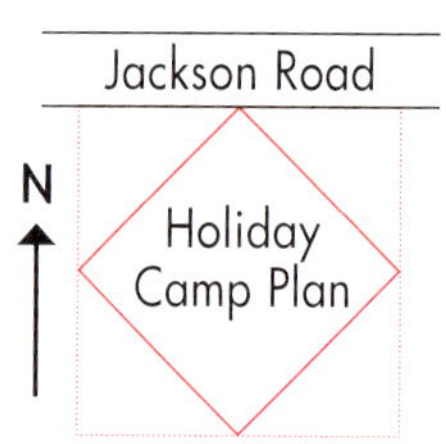

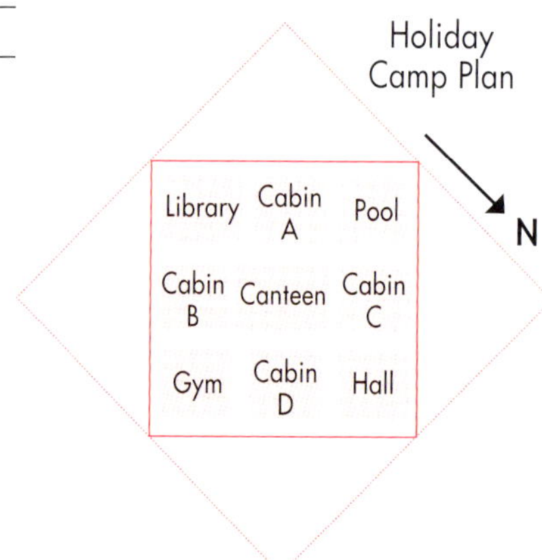

Library ○ Pool ○ Hall ○ Gym ○

JUST IMAGINE!

Some questions can be answered by picturing the result in your mind.

This cube was made by folding this net.
What colour is the face on the right side?

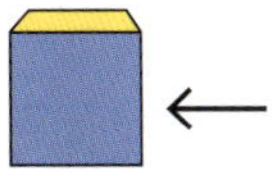

red	green	orange	purple
●	○	○	○

Explanation: Try to imagine the net folded to make the cube. That way you will be able to 'see' the answer. Firstly, the net must be turned around. If the blue face is at the front and the yellow face on top, then the green face will be on the bottom. The face on the right side will be red.

Try this

The minute hand fell off Todd's watch.
What time could it be?

7 o'clock	half past 7
○	○
8 o'clock	**half past 8**
○	○

Imagine where the hands should be for each of the times in the options.

GUESS!

Every question needs to be answered. If you really don't know the answer, or are running out of time, it is alright to have a guess.

If you are making a guess, you might be able to work out that one or two choices are wrong and so have a better chance of guessing correctly.

Sometimes guessing and checking is a way of trying to find an answer. You might make a guess at the answer and then be able to see if that guess is nearly correct. You might then be able to have a better guess. You can continue to guess until you find the right answer.

Daniel bought a kettle and a toaster. Together they cost $122. The kettle costs $14 more than the toaster. How much was the toaster? $54

Explanation:

The kettle cost more than the toaster so the toaster cost less than half of $122.

If the toaster costs $60 the kettle would be $74. But 60 + 74 is more than 122. So the toaster costs less than $60.

If the toaster costs $50 the kettle would be $64. But 50 + 64 is less than 122. So the toaster costs more than $50.

If the toaster costs $55 the kettle would be $69.
Now 55 + 69 = 124. This total is too high, but only just.

If the toaster costs $54 the kettle would cost $68. Now 54 + 68 = 122. This is the right amount. So the toaster must have cost $54.

Note: Another way to do this question is to take the extra cost, $14, away from $122. That leaves $108. The toaster costs half of that.

Try this

Have a guess at the number Robbie might have. Work out how many marbles Thomas would then have and then work out how many Ned would have. Find the total. If the total is less than 38, Robbie must have more marbles. If the total is greater than 38, Robbie will have fewer marbles. If it is exactly 38 you have found the right answer.

Robbie, Thomas and Ned have 38 marbles altogether. Robbie has 4 more marbles than Thomas. Thomas has 1 less marble than Ned.

How many marbles does Ned have?

WEED IT OUT!

It is important to always read the whole question. But sometimes, not all the given information will be needed. You need to be able to decide what is important and what is not.

Ellen collects a stamp on a card every time she spends more than $50 at a shop. When the card is full of stamps, Ellen will be able to choose a gift from the shop. This is Ellen's card.

How many stamps will fit on the card altogether? [24]

Explanation:
We just need to know how many stamps will fit on the card. We can see that 6 stamps fit across the card and 4 stamps fit down the card. So, the number of stamps is $6 \times 4 = 24$.

Molly is making a pattern.
She is using black tiles and white tiles.

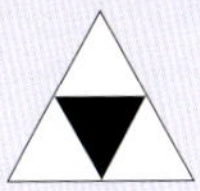

Stage 1
4 tiles

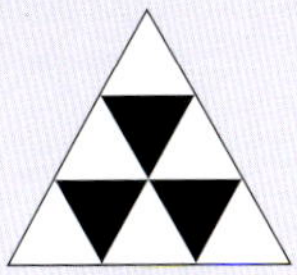

Stage 2
9 tiles

Stage 3
16 tiles

How many white tiles will be needed for stage 5?

15	21	25	36
◯	◯	◯	◯

The question is not asking for the total number of tiles, or the number of black tiles, or the number of white tiles needed for stage 4. All of which have been given as possible options.

Try this

WHAT COULD THE ANSWER BE?

Sometimes there is more than one possible answer to a question. For example, if you are asked to choose a number between 6 and 10 you could choose 7 or 8 or 9. Each of those is a correct answer. So, if you just had to write an answer down, you could choose to write any of those.

In a multiple–choice question, there will be just one of the possible answers given. You will have to work out which one of the choices is correct.

Write a number in the box to make this number sentence correct: $56 - 32 > 4 \times \square$

Explanation: Firstly > means "is greater than".
Now 56 – 32 = 24. So 24 has to be bigger than 4 times the number.

Now 24 is 4 × 6 so the number can be any number that is smaller than 6.

Try this

The medium size must be larger than the small one but smaller than the large one.

Jojo's juice is sold in 3 different sizes: small, medium and large.
The picture shows the small and large sizes.

What size could the medium size be?

4 L	7 L	300 mL	1500 mL
◯	◯	◯	◯

First multiply the number of rows by the number of cars in each row for both Jed and Raj to see how many cars they each have.

Jed and Raj put their toy cars into rows.
Jed has 7 rows and 3 cars in each row.
Raj has 4 rows and 6 cars in each row.
Marco has more cars than Jed but not as many as Raj.

How many cars could Marco have?

20	22	24	26
◯	◯	◯	◯

NO PROBLEM!

Some of the questions, particularly towards the end of the test, will involve problems that need to be solved. Follow these steps:

★ Read the question carefully.

★ Stop and think.

★ Read the question again.

You might be able to find a pattern, work backwards, or use a picture to help you.

A rectangular garden bed has a perimeter of 16 metres. One of the shorter sides is 3 metres long.

How long is each of the longer sides of the garden bed?

5 m

Explanation:

The shape of the garden bed is a rectangle. The opposite sides of a rectangle are the same length. So, two sides are 3 m long.

Now 3 + 3 = 6, so together the two shorter sides add to 6 m.

The perimeter of the rectangle is 16 m.

Now 16 − 6 = 10, so together the two longer sides add to 10 m.

Now half of 10 is 5, so each of the longer sides must be 5 m long.

Try this

This picture shows the position of four buildings in a town.

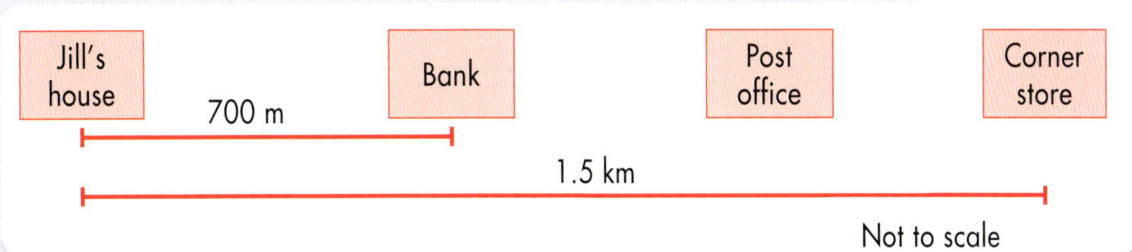

The post office is halfway between the bank and the corner store.

Jill knows that it is 1.5 km from her house to the corner store and 700 m from her house to the bank.

How many metres is it from Jill's house to the post office?

☐ m

First find the distance from the bank to the corner store. The distance from the bank to the post office will be half of that distance.

CHECKLISTS

NUMBERS AND PLACE VALUE

Can you recognise, model and order numbers to tens of thousands? Can you apply place value? Can you partition, rearrange and regroup numbers?

This is an example of partitioning:

18 + 82 = 18 + 2 + 80 = 20 + 80 = 100

Numbers can be added in any order. So, for example, to find 18 + 73 + 82 first add 18 and 82. We know that 18 + 82 = 100 so the question becomes 100 + 73 and the answer is 173.

Try this

Jacob wants to find the answer to 1397 + 864.
Which of these is a way to get the same answer?

1400 + 867	1400 + 861	1390 + 857	1393 + 860
○	●	○	○

Explanation:
There is no need to work out the answer. Use partitioning.

1397 + 864 = 1397 + 3 + 861
= 1400 + 861

Thirty thousand and forty eight is 3 ten thousands, no thousands, no hundreds, 4 tens and 8 ones.

Which number is thirty thousand and forty eight?

3000048	3048	30048	300048
○	○	○	○

There are 6 hundreds, 3 tens and 2 ones.

Which of these is equal to 632?

6 + 3 + 2	600 + 3 + 20	600 + 30 + 2	6 + 30 + 200
○	○	○	○

The largest digit will need to go first.

Isabel has these four number cards. **2** **7** **5** **8**

What is the largest number that Isabel can make with these cards? ☐

WORKING WITH NUMBERS

Can you identify even and odd numbers and use their properties? Can you use estimation and rounding? Can you identify which operation to use?

The four main operations are addition, subtraction, multiplication and division. You need to read the question carefully to be sure that you are using the correct operation. You can use estimation to help you decide. Always stop to think if your answer makes sense.

The number of litres of milk produced at a dairy is recorded. Here are the results for 3 days this week.

Monday 5058 Tuesday 5196 Wednesday 4921

Which is the best way to estimate the total litres for the three days?

5000 + 5000 + 5000 ◯ 5000 + 5200 + 4900 ◯

5100 + 5200 + 4900 ⬤ 5100 + 5200 + 5000 ◯

Explanation:

Round each of the amounts to the nearest hundred.
5058 is closer to 5100 than 5000
5196 is closer to 5200 than 5100
4921 is closer to 4900 than 5000
So, of the choices, the best estimate is 5100 + 5200 + 4900.

Note: The amounts can also be estimated by rounding to the nearest 1000 so 5000 + 5000 + 5000 is a possible estimation, but 5100 + 5200 + 4900 is a better estimation

Try this

How many whole numbers are between 12 and 44? What fraction of those will be odd?

How many odd numbers are between 12 and 44?

14 ◯ 15 ◯ 16 ◯ 17 ◯

Kane has 17 more football cards than Edward. Kane has 83 cards. How can you work out how many cards Edward has?

Add 17 to 83 ◯ Subtract 17 from 83 ◯

Multiply 17 by 83 ◯ Divide 83 by 17 ◯

The number of cards that Edward has is 17 fewer than 83.

ADDITION AND SUBTRACTION

Can you recall addition facts and related subtraction facts for single digit numbers? Can you use various strategies to add and subtract numbers? Can you solve problems using addition or subtraction?

Being able to quickly add and subtract single numbers is a really important skill!

Ali, Zara and Tom share 35 marbles. Zara got 4 more marbles than Tom. Ali got 1 more marble than Tom.

How many marbles did Tom get? [10]

Explanation:

4 + 1 = 5. So, altogether Zara and Ali got 5 more marbles than Tom.

Now 35 – 5 = 30. So, if Zara and Ali did not have any extra marbles, they would have shared 30 equally. 30 ÷ 3 = 10. So Tom got 10 marbles.

Note: With problems, it is often possible to check the answer. If Tom got 10 marbles, Ali got 11 and Zara got 14. Now 10 + 11 + 14 = 35. So, the answer must be correct.

Try this

What do you need to add to 38 to get 40?

38 + 25 = [ ]

To find the difference we subtract the smaller number from the larger one.

There are 1320 sheep on a farm.
There are 565 cows on the farm.

What is the difference between the number of sheep and the number of cows on the farm?

755	1245	865	1885
◯	◯	◯	◯

First work out what digit must follow 8 in the second number. So, looking at the last digits 7 + what number = 13 (it can't add to 3 so it must be 13).

Write one number in each empty box to make this number sentence correct.

1		7	+	8		=	2	4	3

MULTIPLICATION

Can you recall multiplication facts for numbers up to 10 × 10? Can you represent and solve problems involving multiplication?

Learning your multiplication tables is probably the most important thing you can do to help with your maths!

Maddie has 3 boxes of long pencils. There are 6 long pencils in each box. Maddie also has 5 boxes of short pencils. There are 9 short pencils in each box.

How many pencils does Maddie have altogether?

63	69	57	23
●	○	○	○

Explanation:

Number of long pencils = 3 × 6
= 18

Number of short pencils = 5 × 9
= 45

Total = 18 + 45
= 63

So, Maddie has 63 pencils altogether.

Try this

Lily has 8 packets of ribbons.
There are 6 ribbons in every packet.
How many ribbons does Lily have? ☐

Multiply 8 by 6.

Which gives the same answer as 9 × 4?

7 × 5	6 × 6	10 × 3	5 × 8
○	○	○	○

Work out the answer to each multiplication.

There are 8 classes at Michael's school. Each class has between 15 and 20 students. Which could be the number of students at Michael's school?

80	110	130	170
○	○	○	○

The smallest possible number would be 8 × 15.
The largest possible number would be 8 × 20.

DIVISION

Can you recall division facts related to multiplication facts up to 10 × 10? Can you use mental and written strategies with division and solve problems?

Division is the opposite of multiplication. So, for example, because 7 × 4 = 28 it follows that 28 ÷ 4 = 7 and 28 ÷ 7 = 4.

There are 30 balloons in a packet. Four friends share the balloons equally and there are some left over.

What is the smallest number of balloons that could be left over?

1	2	3	4
○	●	○	○

Explanation:
30 divided by 4 is 7 remainder 2. So the friends would each have 7 balloons and there would be 2 left over.

How many times does 5 go into 6? How many are left over? So how many times does 5 go into 10?

6015 ÷ 5 =

1023	1203	123	1230
○	○	○	○

Divide 78 by 6.

Alison is packing cans into boxes.
Each box holds 6 cans.
How many boxes will Alison need for 78 cans? ☐

Divide 6 into 48.

Oliver is cutting pizzas into 6 pieces like this.

Oliver wants to have 48 pieces.

How many pizzas will he need? ☐

FRACTIONS AND DECIMALS

Do you understand equivalent fractions? Can you count by quarters, halves or thirds? Can you locate fractions on a number line? Do you understand place value with tenths and hundredths? Can you make connections between fractional and decimal notations?

A decimal is a fraction with denominator a power of ten. So 0.9, for example is $\frac{9}{10}$ and 0.07 is $\frac{7}{100}$.

What fraction is at the position on the number line marked by the arrow?

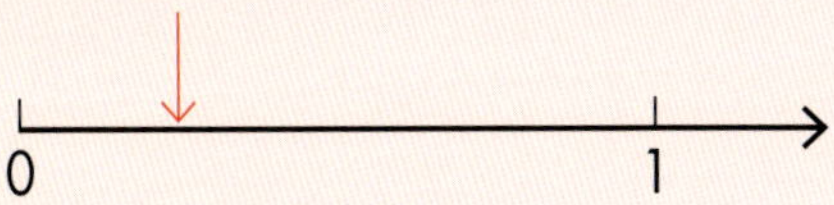

$\frac{1}{2}$ ○ $\frac{1}{8}$ ○ $\frac{1}{3}$ ○ $\frac{1}{4}$ ● (answer)

Explanation:
Imagine the number line divided into equal parts.

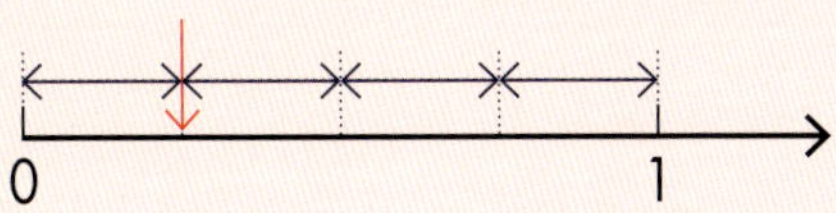

Four of those parts fit into 1 whole. So each part is $\frac{1}{4}$.
The position marked by the arrow is $\frac{1}{4}$.

Try this

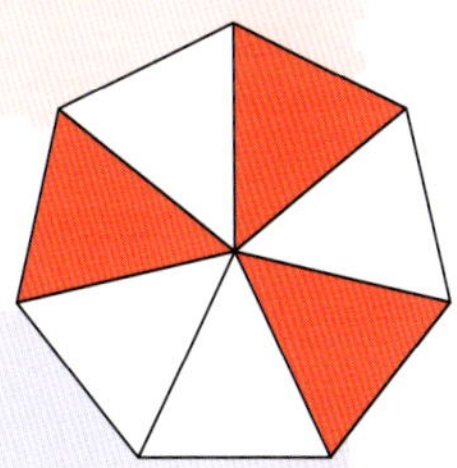

What fraction of this shape is shaded red?

$\frac{1}{2}$ ○ $\frac{3}{7}$ ○ $\frac{4}{7}$ ○ $\frac{3}{4}$ ○

How many sectors are shaded red? How many sectors are there altogether?

4.07 is equal to:

4 + 0.7 ○ 4 + 0.07 ○ 0.4 + 0.07 ○ 0.7 + 0.4 ○

There are 4 ones, no tenths and 7 hundredths.

MONEY

Can you represent money values in many ways? Can you count amounts of money? Can you solve problems involving purchases and working out the amount of change?

Remember that change must be calculated to the nearest five cents.

At a garden shop, small plants are for sale for $3 each or 4 for $10. Sandy buys 10 of the plants.
How much should she pay?

$24	$26	$28	$30
○	●	○	○

Explanation:
Sandy can get any 4 plants for $10 so she can get 8 plants for $20. She wants 2 more plants and they will cost $3 each. Now $2 \times 3 = 6$.

Total cost = $20 + $6 = $26

What must be added to $34.95 to make $35.00? Then how many more dollars are needed to make $50.00?

Rachel buys a book for $34.95.
How much change does she get from $50.00?

$15.50	$16.50	$15.05	$16.05
○	○	○	○

Try this

Ron has just these coins.

He buys a sandwich for $2.40.
How much money does Ron have left?

40 cents	45 cents	50 cents	55 cents
○	○	○	○

Think about which coins Ron could use to pay for his sandwich.
He will need change.

PATTERNS

Can you describe, continue and create number patterns? Can you solve problems involving patterns with objects or numbers?

The numbers in number patterns are called terms. Look at the difference between the following terms to find the pattern. In patterns with objects, look to see how many objects are repeated.

Sally is making a pattern with triangles.

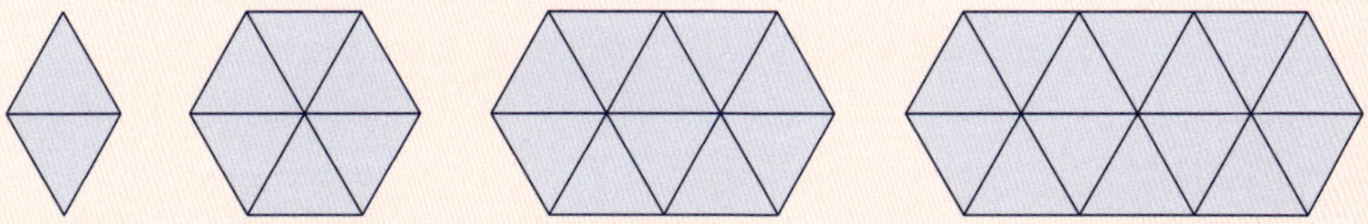

Shape 1	Shape 2	Shape 3	Shape 4
2 triangles	6 triangles	10 triangles	14 triangles

How many triangles will Sally need for shape 6?

18 ○ 20 ○ 22 ● 24 ○

Explanation:

2 + 4 = 6; 6 + 4 = 10; 10 + 4 = 14

Each shape has 4 more triangles than the shape before.

So shape 5 will have 14 + 4 = 18 triangles.

Shape 6 will have 18 + 4 = 22 triangles.

Try this

53, 46, 39, 32, ?

What is the next number in this pattern? ☐

What number must be taken away each time to get the next number?

Tim put his ropes in order of their length. The lengths make a pattern.

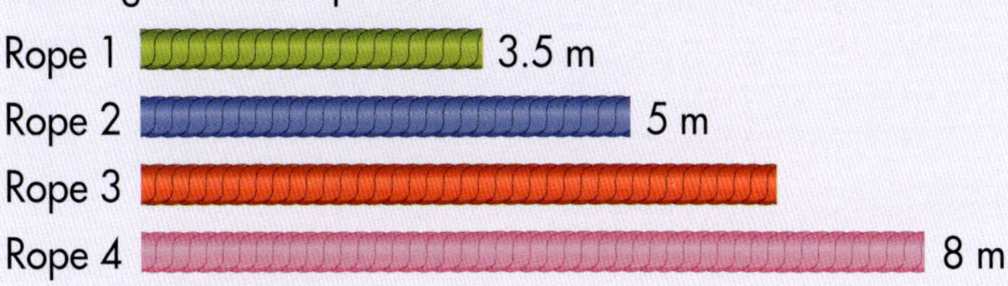

What is the length of rope 3?

5.5 m ○ 6 m ○ 6.5 m ○ 7.5 m ○

How much longer is rope 2 than rope 1?

MEASUREMENT

Can you measure, order and compare objects?
Are you familiar with units of length, mass and capacity?
Can you use scaled instruments?

The size of something can be estimated with informal measurements. The standard unit of length is the metre. The standard unit of mass is the kilogram and the standard unit of capacity is the litre. 'milli' means one thousandth and 'kilo' means one thousand.

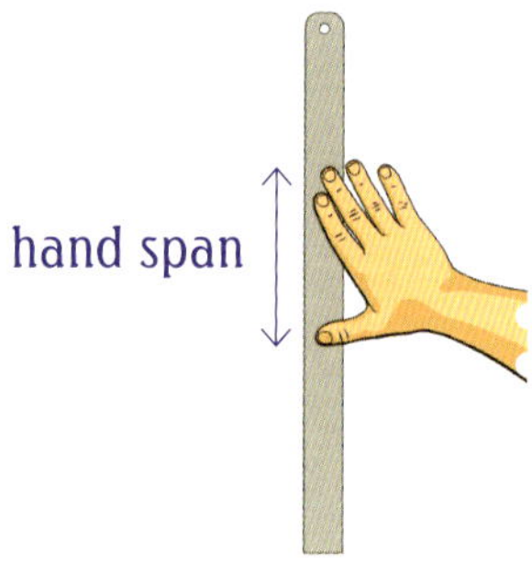

Jack knows that his hand span measures about 20 cm. He measures the length of a table and finds it to be just short of 8 hand spans.

The length of the table is about:

28 cm	100 cm	150 cm	280 cm
○	○	●	○

Explanation: There are nearly 8 hand spans and each one is about 20 cm long. Now $8 \times 20 = 160$. So the length of the table is a little bit less than 160 cm.

Of the choices, the length of the table could be 150 cm.

Try this

What would you use to measure the mass of the drum?

Which of these units could be used to measure the mass of a drum of oil?

metres	litres	kilograms	seconds
○	○	○	○

Where would the one litre measurement be on the jug?

How much juice is in this jug?

50 mL	250 mL
○	○
500 mL	**1500 mL**
○	○

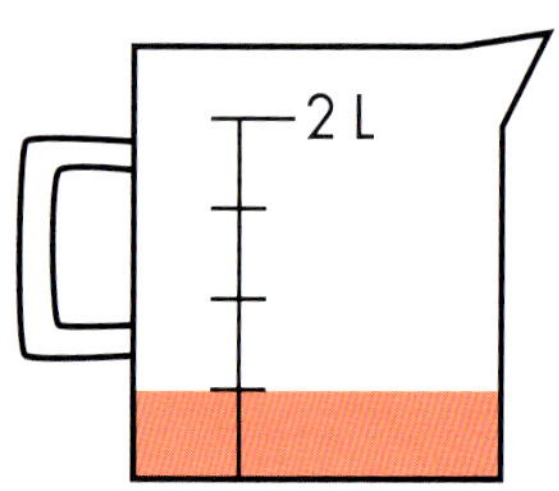

TIME

Can you tell time to the minute? Do you understand the relationship between units of time? Can you solve simple time problems?

There are 60 seconds in a minute and 60 minutes in an hour. There are 24 hours in a day. We use am to show times in the morning (before noon) and pm for times in the afternoon (after noon and before midnight).

Jay left home at 8:30 am to go to school. He got home again at 4:00 pm. How long was Jay away from home?

$4\frac{1}{2}$ hours	6 hours	$6\frac{1}{2}$ hours	$7\frac{1}{2}$ hours
○	○	○	●

Explanation:
From 8:30 to 9:00 is half an hour. From 9 am to 12 noon is 3 hours. From 12 noon until 4 pm is 4 hours.
So altogether Jay is away for $7\frac{1}{2}$ hours.

Try this

This notice is shown at the station.

At what time does the next train leave?

4:15	4:03	3:20	3:04
○	○	○	○

The minute hand is on the 3; the hour hand is just past 4.

This is the bus timetable.

Newtown	7:24 am	7:35 am	7:51 am	8:17 am	8:44 am
Gum Scrub	7:37 am	7:49 am	8:02 am	8:28 am	8:58 am
Bonny Bay	7:55 am	8:07 am	8:24 am	8:50 am	9:16 am
City	8:08 am	8:21 am	8:37 am	9:03 am	9:29 am

Elsie knows that if she catches the 8:44 am bus from Newtown she will get to the city at 9:29 am.
She needs to be in the city by 9:00 am tomorrow morning.
What time should she catch the bus in Newtown?

7:24 am	7:35 am	7:51 am	8:17 am
○	○	○	○

Look in the last row to find a time before 9:00 am.

PERIMETER, AREA AND VOLUME

Do you know what is meant by perimeter? Can you compare areas of regular shapes and irregular shapes? Can you find the perimeter and area of rectangles? Can you compare volumes of objects?

Perimeter is the distance around the outside of a shape. Area is the amount of space inside a 2D shape. Volume is the amount of space inside a 3D object.

Which rectangle has the largest area?

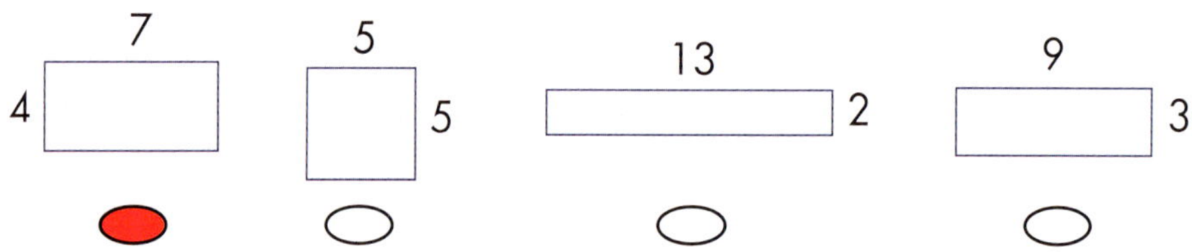

Explanation:

To find the area of a rectangle we multiply the length by the width.

$7 \times 4 = 28$ $5 \times 5 = 25$ $13 \times 2 = 26$ $9 \times 3 = 27$

So, the largest area is 28 square units.

Try this

Count by 20s.

Cody has used 10 tiles to cover the top of a table.

Each tile is a square of side length 20 cm.

What is the perimeter of the tabletop?

140 cm 200 cm 240 cm 280 cm

Because the object is going to be a cube there must be the same number of blocks in each of the three dimensions.

Paul is building a cube with small blocks.

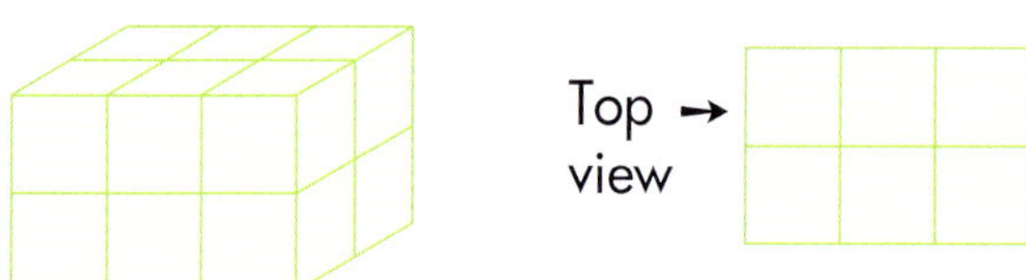

What is the smallest number of extra blocks Paul needs?

SHAPES

Can you identify 2D shapes? Do you know what it means for two lines to be parallel?

You should know the names of all the common shapes and recognise them. Parallel lines are lines on the same flat surface that never meet.

Liam divided this shape by drawing two parallel lines.

The centre part is a rectangle. What are the two other shapes?

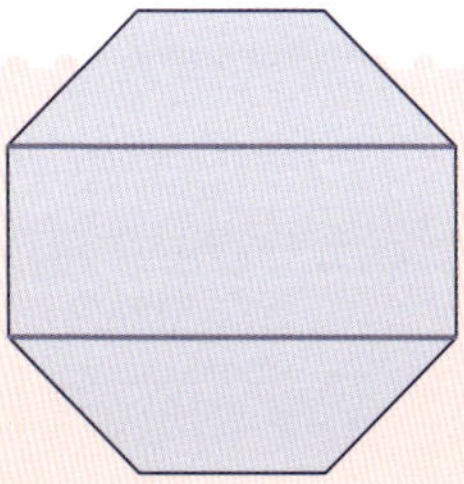

hexagons	trapeziums	parallelograms	rectangles
○	●	○	○

Explanation:
The two shapes are the same. Each has four sides so it is not a hexagon. It only has one pair of opposite sides parallel, so it is not a parallelogram or a rectangle. It is a trapezium.

Try this

Which of these shapes is a hexagon?

A hexagon has 6 sides.

○ A ○ B ○ C ○ D

Which of these shapes does not have any parallel sides?

Parallel sides never meet, even if they were continued forever.

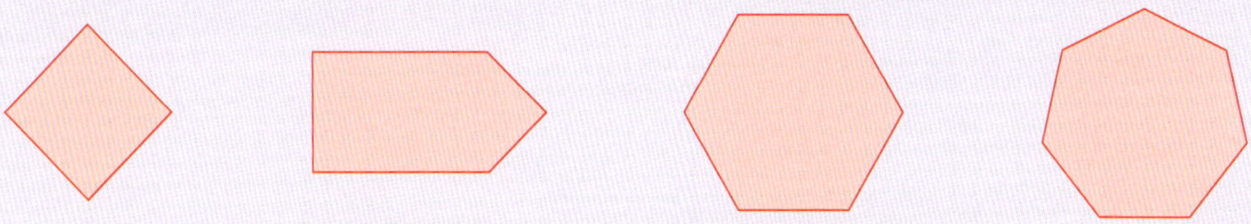

○ A ○ B ○ C ○ D

OBJECTS

Can you describe key features of 3D objects? Can you connect 3D objects with their nets and with views from the top, front or side?

You need to know the names of common objects and recognise them. You need to know how many faces, edges and vertices they have and what each face looks like.

These shapes are the five faces of which 3D object?

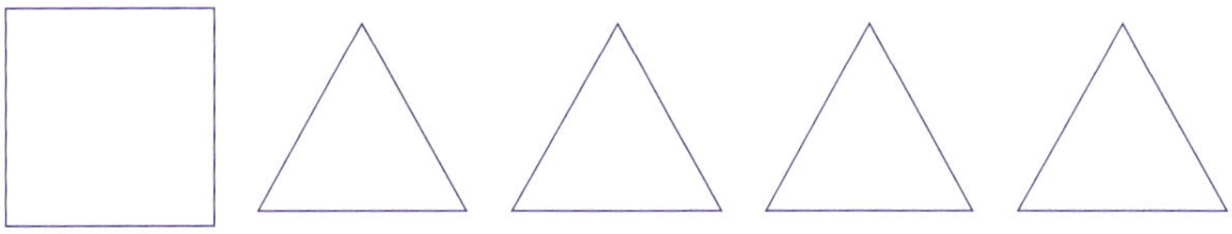

triangular prism ○ | triangular pyramid ○ | square pyramid ● | pentagonal prism ○

Explanation:

Consider the choices:

A triangular prism has 2 triangular faces and 3 rectangular faces.

A triangular pyramid has 4 triangular faces.

A square pyramid has 1 square face and 4 triangular faces.

A pentagonal prism has 2 pentagonal faces and 5 rectangular faces.

So the object is a square pyramid.

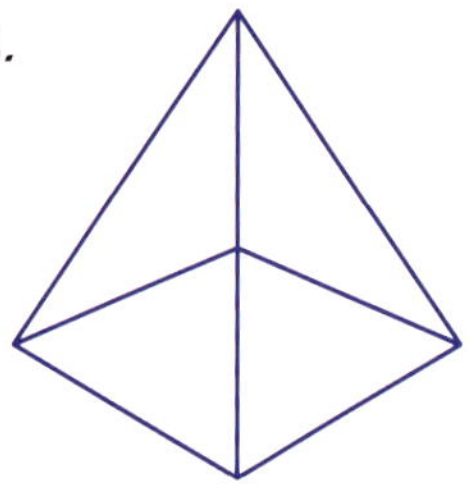

Imagine folding each of the options. Do they make a cube?

Which is NOT the net of a cube?

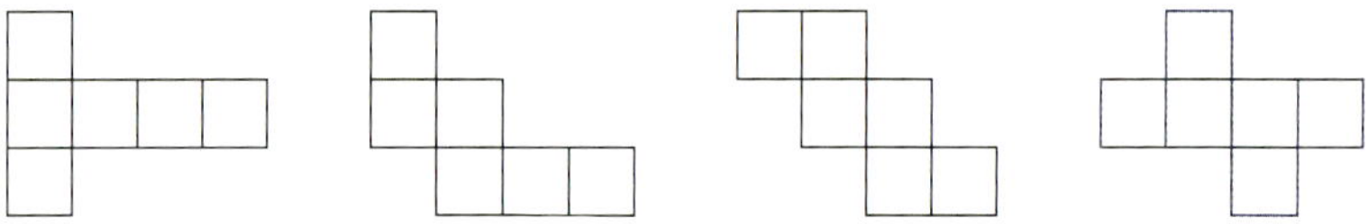

A ○ B ○ C ○ D ○

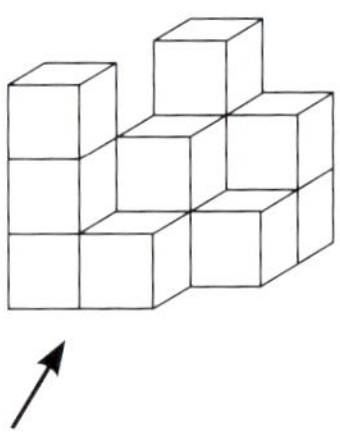

front

How many rows of blocks? How many blocks in each row?

This object was built from 12 blocks.
What is the view from the front?

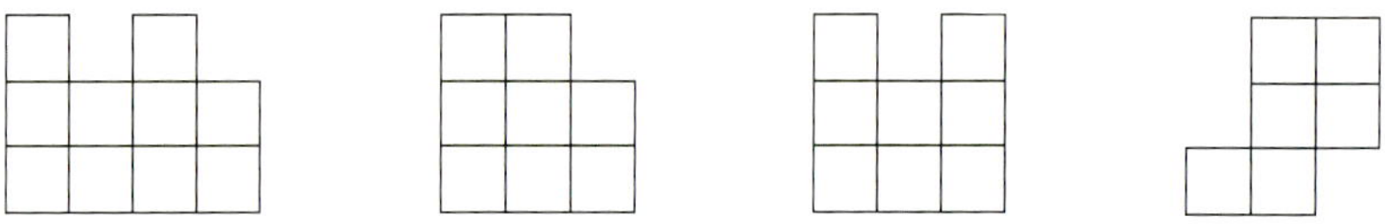

A ○ B ○ C ○ D ○

LOCATION

Do you understand simple grid maps? Can you use simple scales, legends and directions to find information relating to maps? Do you understand the main compass directions?

On a grid map, a position is named by coordinates. The horizontal coordinate (often a letter) is given first and then the vertical coordinate. You should be able to place the directions south, east and west when given north, as well as the directions between each of those such as north-east.

The picture shows a plan of the beds in wards A, B, C and D of a hospital. There are 6 more wards on this floor, all numbered using the same pattern.

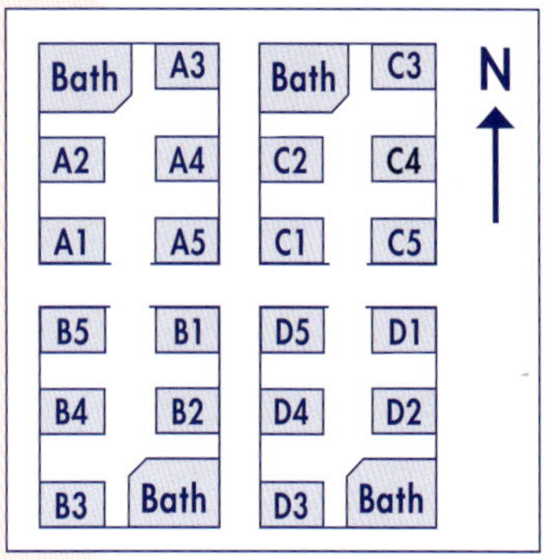

Joe is in the hospital.
His bed is in the north-east corner of ward H.

What is the number of Joe's bed?

H1 (filled) — H2 — H3 — H5

Explanation:
Following the pattern, wards E, G and I would be on the north side and wards F, H and J on the south side. On the south side the first bed is in the north-east corner. So, Joe would be in bed H1.

Try this

Zane leaves the park and walks west in Main Street. At the next street he turns right.

Where might Zane be going?

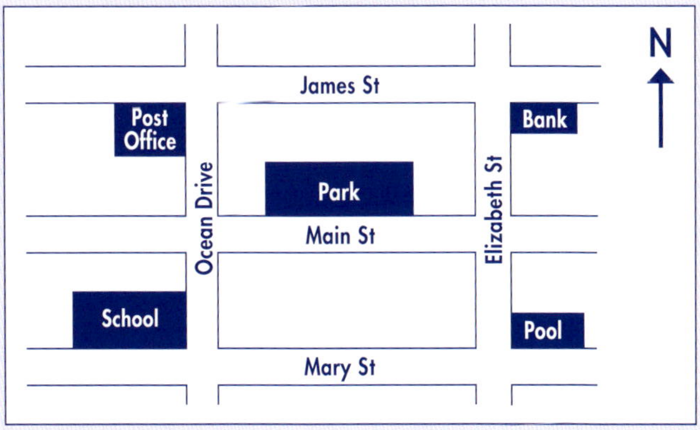

Post Office — Bank — Pool — School

Imagine yourself following the directions.

SYMMETRY AND TRANSFORMATION

Can you identify symmetry in the environment? Can you make symmetrical patterns? Can you identify line and rotational symmetries? Can you describe translations (slides), reflections (flips) and rotations (turns) of 2D shapes? Do you understand enlargement?

A shape has line symmetry if you can fold it along the line and the two parts match exactly. It will have rotational symmetry if it can be turned around a central point, half a turn say, and look the same as it did.

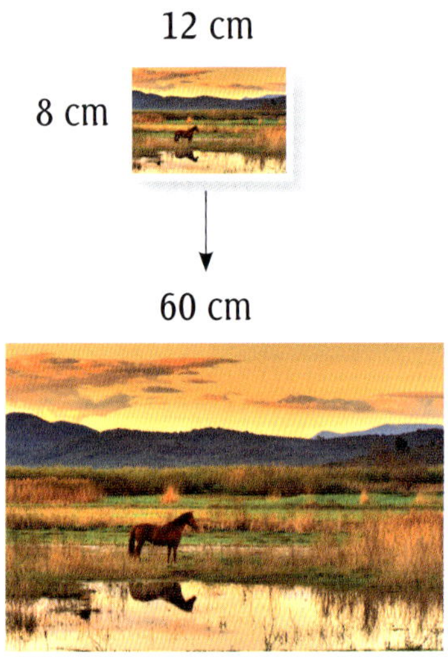

Jenny had one of her photographs enlarged.

How wide is the enlarged photo? 40 cm

Explanation:
The photo was 12 cm long and is now 60 cm long.
Now $60 \div 12 = 5$. So the photo is 5 times longer.
It must also be 5 times wider. $8 \times 5 = 40$.
So the photo is now 40 cm wide.

Try this

Imagine the picture flipped over the dotted line.

Which picture shows a reflection over the dotted line?

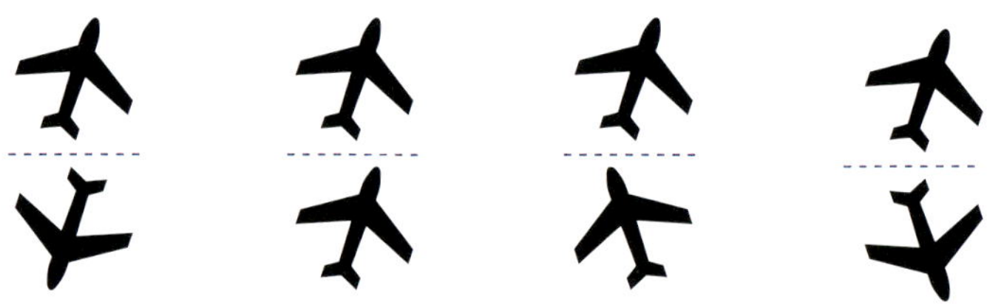

A B C D

Which of these shapes has exactly 2 lines of symmetry?

Where can each shape be folded so that the 2 pieces match exactly?

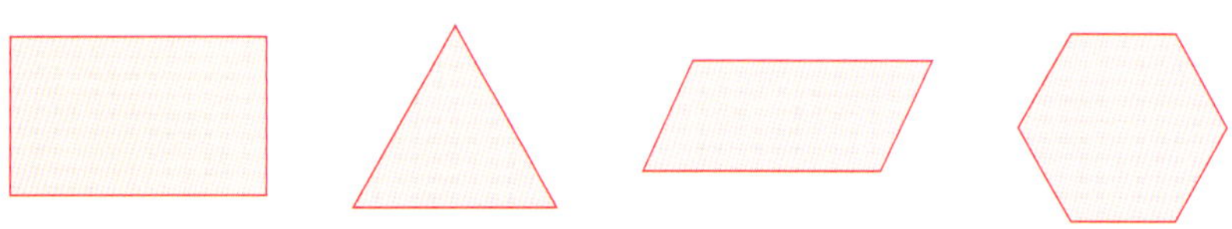

A B C D

ANGLES

Can you understand that angles are measures of turn? Can you compare angles? Can you estimate angle size? Can you measure angles using a protractor? Can you identify right angles, acute angles, obtuse and reflex angles?

A right angle is a quarter turn. A right angle measures 90°. An acute angle is smaller than a right angle. It measures less than 90°. A straight angle is a half turn. It measures 180°. An obtuse angle is larger than a right angle but smaller than a straight angle. It measures between 90° and 180°. A full turn is 360°. A reflex angle measures between 180° and 360°.

Which angle is closest to 80° in size?

Explanation:
A right angle measures 90°. An angle measuring 80° will be slightly smaller than a right angle.

Try this

Which angle is the largest?

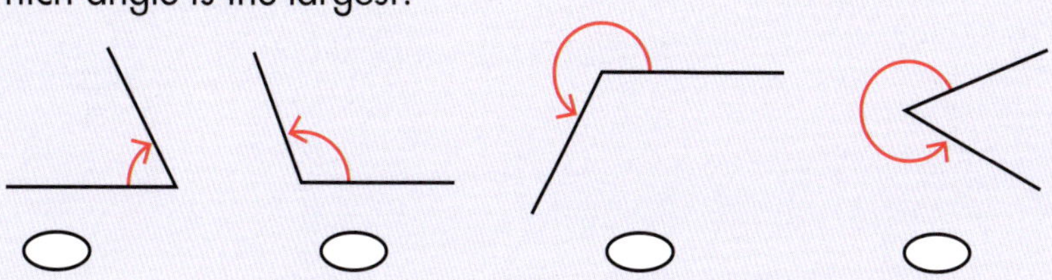

A B C D

Which arm has turned furthest from its matching arm?

Which triangle has an obtuse angle?

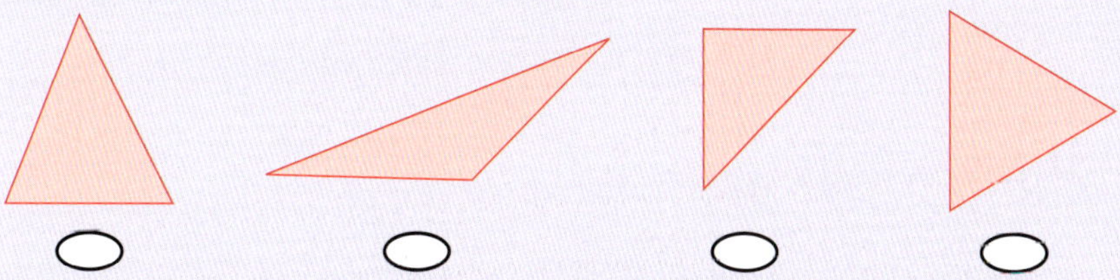

A B C D

An obtuse angle is larger than a right angle.

CHANCE

Can you describe outcomes of chance experiments? Can you order the chances of outcomes occurring? Do you understand that in some events the chance of something happening will not be affected by what happened before? Can you use fractions to represent the probability of an outcome?

If outcomes are equally likely to occur, then the chance of an event is equal to the number of times that event occurs out of the total number of outcomes. For example, if there are 7 balls in a bag and 3 of them are red, then the chance of choosing a red ball is 3 out of 7 or $\frac{3}{7}$.

Ella rolls a normal dice 3 times.
It shows 5 each time.
Then Ella rolls the dice again.

Which statement is true about the dice?

It is certain to show 5. ◯	It is certain not to show 5. ◯
It is likely to show 5. ◯	It is unlikely to show 5. ●

Explanation:
The result of a previous roll of the dice will not affect the next roll. So it doesn't matter what Ella rolled before. There are 6 numbers on the dice and only one of those is a 5, so rolling a 5 is unlikely.

Try this

It is least likely to stop on the smallest sector.

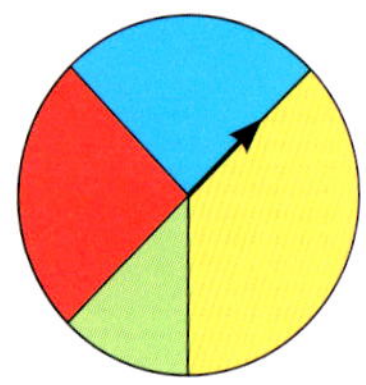

Toby spins this spinner.
On which colour is it least likely to stop?

Blue	Red	Yellow	Green
◯	◯	◯	◯

How many marbles of each colour are in the box?

Holly has these marbles in a box.
She takes out 3 marbles. Which is impossible?

3 blue marbles ◯	1 green and 2 red marbles ◯
1 blue and 2 yellow marbles ◯	1 blue, 1 green and 1 yellow ◯

DATA

Can you understand that there are different methods of data collection? Can you compare different data sets? Can you read and interpret information presented in data displays?

You must be able to read and understand tables, picture graphs and column graphs.

Martin recorded this data about his family's vehicles.

TYPE	COLOUR	AGE (years)	MONTH OF REGISTRATION
Car	white	4	June
Ute	black	3	August
Truck	white	7	October
Car	blue	1	November

How did Martin order his data?

By type ◯ By colour ◯ By age ◯ By month of registration ⬤

Explanation:

Look at each column to see if there is any order. Under type, there is a car first and last so the vehicles are not in order by type. Under colour white appears twice, but not together. The vehicles are not in order by colour. Under age the numbers are not in increasing or decreasing order. The vehicles are not in order by age. Under month of registration, the months are in order as they occur during the year. The vehicles must be in order of month of registration.

Try this

At a show ribbons were awarded for novelty events. Some ribbons were blue and the rest were gold.

This graph shows the number of ribbons won by some children in a family.

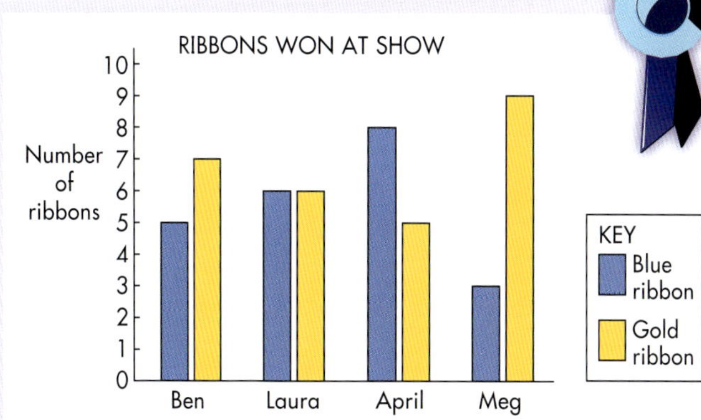

Who won the most ribbons?

Ben ◯ Laura ◯ April ◯ Meg ◯

Add the number of blue ribbons to the number of gold ribbons for each child.

NUMERACY PRACTICE TEST

The test is 50 minutes.
All questions should be answered using a 2B or HB pencil.
You are not allowed to use any calculator for this test.

1. What time does this clock show?

5:15	5:03	3:05	3:25
◯	◯	◯	◯
A	B	C	D

2. Alice had 14 jellybeans. She ate 3 and gave 5 to Jo.
How many jellybeans does Alice have left? ☐

3. Which number is six thousand and twenty four?

600024	6240	6024	60024
◯	◯	◯	◯
A	B	C	D

4. Toby has these coins.

He buys a chocolate for $2.35.
How much money does Toby have left?

$1.40	$1.60	$2.40	$2.60
◯	◯	◯	◯
A	B	C	D

5. Which shape will look the same when flipped over the dotted line?

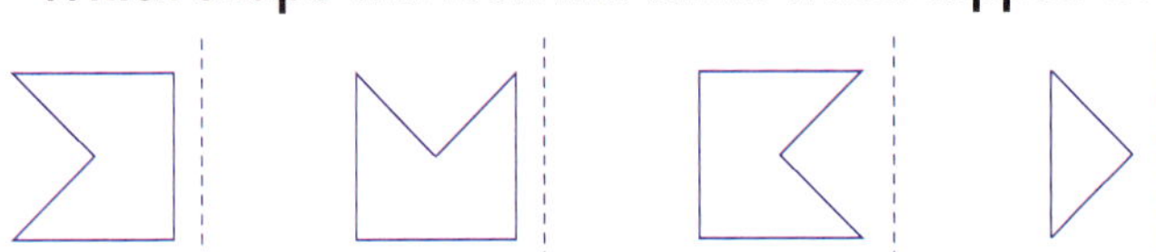

◯	◯	◯	◯
A	B	C	D

6.  **This 3D object is a:**

prism	cone	cylinder	pyramid
◯	◯	◯	◯
A	B	C	D

7. Some students voted for year representative.
The results were shown in a table.

Student	Billy	Jade	Sam	Ali	Max	Kate
Number of votes	38	52	19	61	45	27

Who got fewer votes than Jade but more votes than Billy?

Sam	Ali	Max	Kate
⬭	⬭	⬭	⬭
A	B	C	D

8. Which shows an acute angle?

⬭	⬭	⬭	⬭
A	B	C	D

9. What fraction of this flag is blue?

$\frac{2}{3}$	$\frac{2}{5}$	$\frac{3}{5}$	$\frac{1}{2}$
⬭	⬭	⬭	⬭
A	B	C	D

10. What is the length of this pencil?

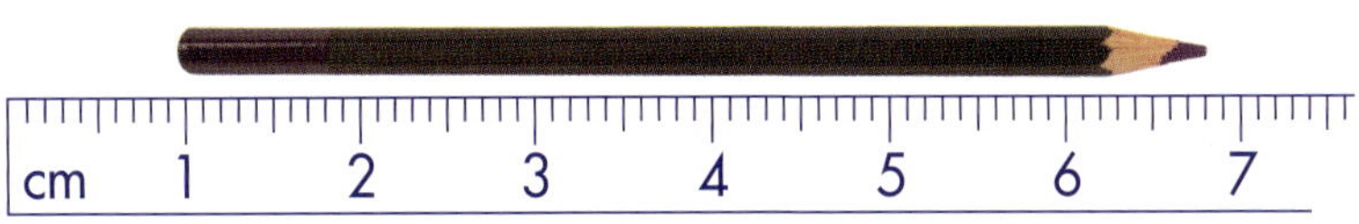

58 mm	53 mm	63 mm	68 mm
⬭	⬭	⬭	⬭
A	B	C	D

11. 1998 + 543 = 2000 + ☐

12. 2, 3, 5, 8, 12, 17, 23, ?
What is the next number in this pattern?

27	28	29	30
⬭	⬭	⬭	⬭
A	B	C	D

13. Henry puts his toy cars and his toy trucks in 2 rows like this.

Each toy car is 8 cm long. How long is each toy truck?

14 cm	15 cm	16 cm	18 cm
⬭	⬭	⬭	⬭
A	B	C	D

14. What number is at the position marked by the arrow on this number line?

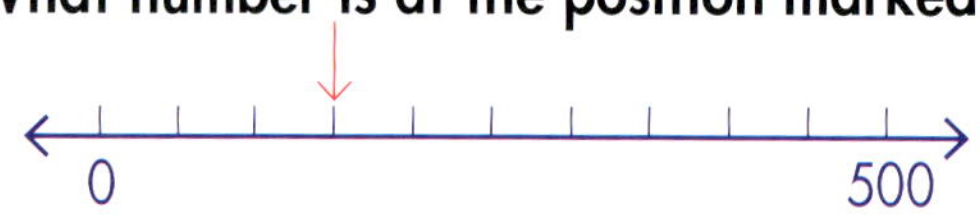

50	100	150	200
⬭	⬭	⬭	⬭
A	B	C	D

15. 5.27 is equal to:

$5 + 0.2 + 0.07$	$5 + 0.02 + 0.7$	$7 + 0.2 + 0.05$	$7 + 0.02 + 0.5$
⬭	⬭	⬭	⬭
A	B	C	D

16. These were the top five colours of new cars sold in Carland last year.

COLOUR	NUMBER OF CARS
White	628
Silver	539
Red	417
Blue	285
Black	244

Which statement is true for a new car sold in Carland last year?

A ⬭ It is certain to be white.

B ⬭ It is more likely to be red than silver.

C ⬭ It is less likely to be black than blue.

D ⬭ It is impossible to be green.

17. A river cruise was held for 48 people.
The cost of the cruise was $5 per person.
What was the total cost of the cruise? $ ______

18. Which of these is NOT the net of a pyramid?

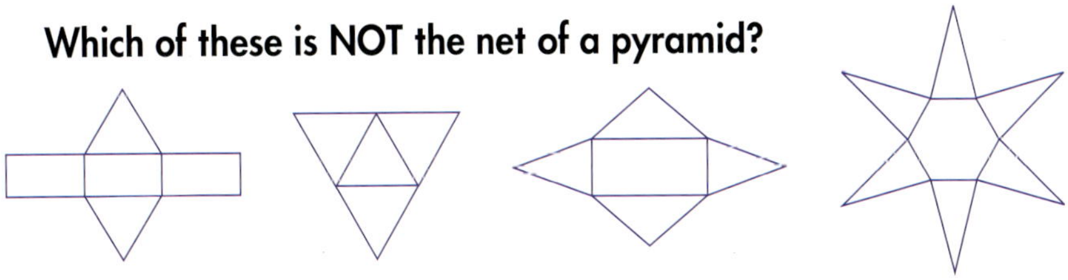

A B C D

19. Emma got on the train at 4:37 pm. She got off the train at 5:11 pm. For how many minutes was Emma on the train?

26	34	48	74
A	B	C	D

20. Mary shades some squares on this grid. When she finishes, the pattern has one line of symmetry.

How will the square G3 be shaded?

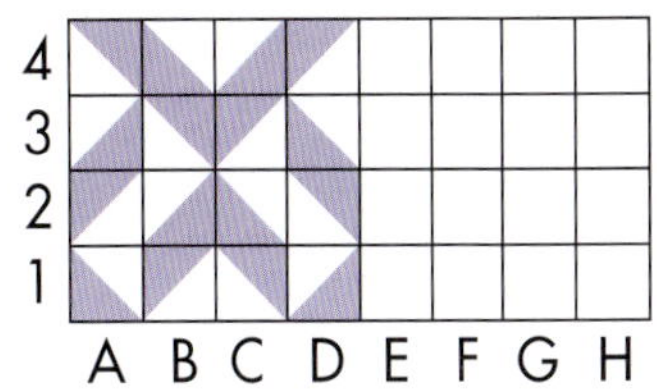

A

B

C

D

21. What is the perimeter of this paddock?

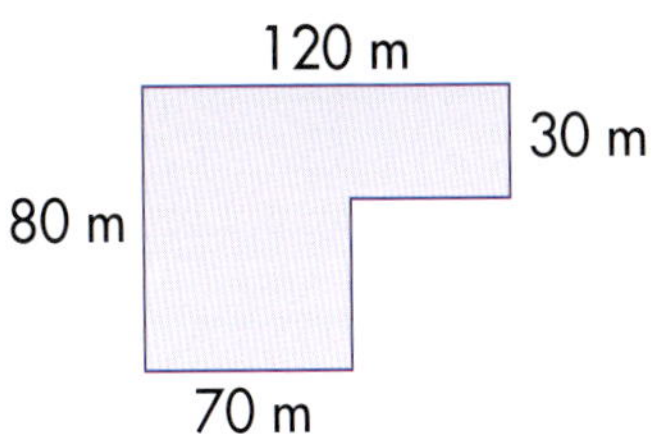

200 m	300 m	350 m	400 m
A	B	C	D

22. This graph shows the number of students in each year 5 class at a school.

Which class has the most girls?

5D	5K
A	B
5M	5W
C	D

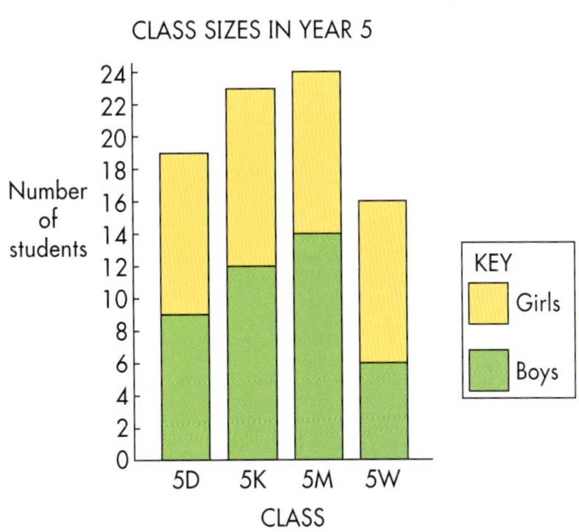

23. There are 120 animals on a farm. One quarter of the animals are cows. One third of the cows have calves.

How many cows on the farm have calves? [ ]

24. This arrow will be rotated a quarter of a turn: 
What could it look like after the rotation?

 ○ A

 ○ B

 ○ C

 ○ D

25. Sammi copied a picture of a car onto a grid. Each unit on the grid represented 42 cm.

What is the length of the real car?

[ ] cm

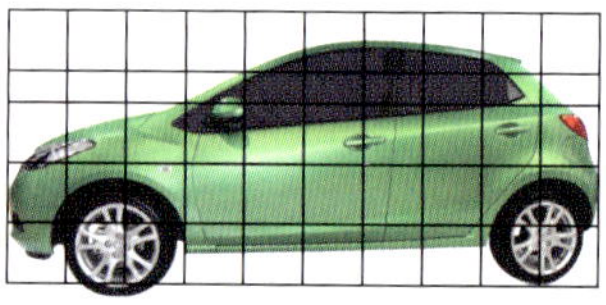

↔ 1 unit

26. Stephanie keeps her medals in 12 boxes.
9 boxes hold 5 medals each. The other boxes hold 8 medals each.

How many medals does Stephanie have? [ ]

27. Mr Lee drives west in Gordon St.
After crossing the highway he turns into the next street on the left.

Which street is Mr Lee now in?

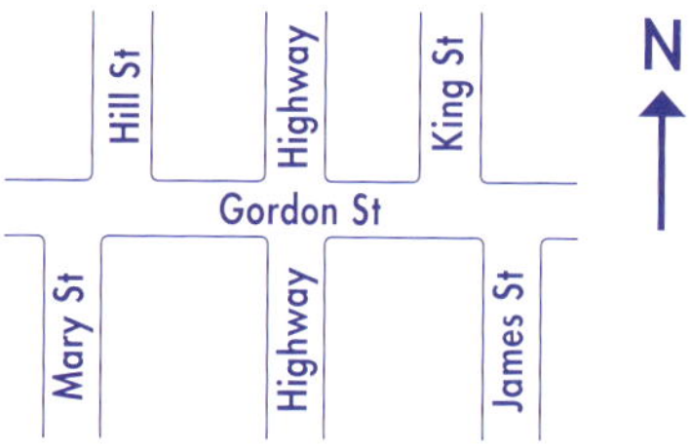

Mary St	Hill St	King St	James St
○	○	○	○
A	B	C	D

28. Paris started with a number. She halved it and then added 7.
Her answer was 11. What number did Paris start with?

2	4	8	9
○	○	○	○
A	B	C	D

29. Tia puts beads on a string making a pattern.

○□•□•◉•◉•□○□•□•◉•◉•□○□•□•◉•◉•□ …

How many • does Tia need for each ○?

1	2	3	4
○	○	○	○
A	B	C	D

30. This 3D object was made from 12 cubes. It was then painted blue.

How many of the 12 cubes have exactly two faces that are blue?

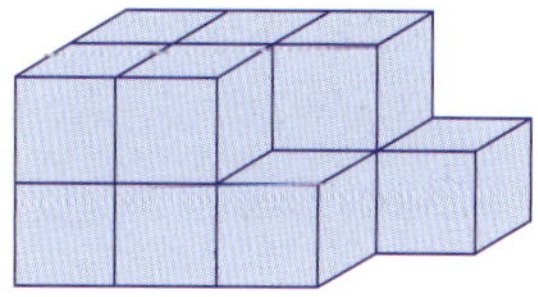

1	2	3	4
⬭	⬭	⬭	⬭
A	B	C	D

31. In 6 years time Clint will be twice as old as Jay. If Jay is 9 years old now, how old is Clint?

32. How many lines of symmetry does this design have?

2	4	6	8
⬭	⬭	⬭	⬭
A	B	C	D

33. How many millilitres of juice are in this jug?

700	750	70	75
⬭	⬭	⬭	⬭
A	B	C	D

34. Sue went to her doctor on April 13. She has to go back to her doctor exactly 6 weeks later.

When does Sue have to go to the doctor?

May 22	May 23	May 24	May 25
⬭	⬭	⬭	⬭
A	B	C	D

MAY

S	M	T	W	T	F	S
	1	2	3	4	5	6
7	8	9	10	11	12	13
14	15	16	17	18	19	20
21	22	23	24	25	26	27
28	29	30	31			

35. This pie graph was drawn to show the favourite pet of 200 students.

About how many students chose cat as their favourite?

Favourite Pet

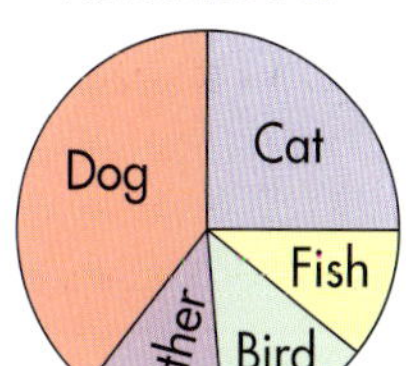

20	50	75	100
⬭	⬭	⬭	⬭
A	B	C	D

36. Jesse makes 60 cupcakes. He puts them in trays like this. Which of these shows how Jesse could work out how many trays he needs?

$60 + 12$	$60 - 12$	60×12	$60 \div 12$
○	○	○	○
A	B	C	D

37. Which gives the best chance of getting a red ball?

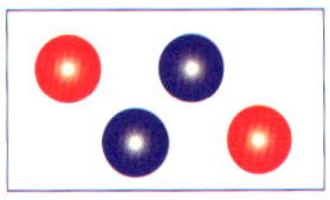	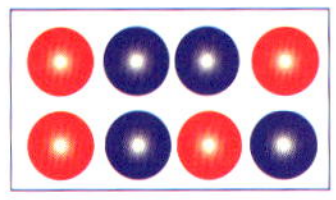	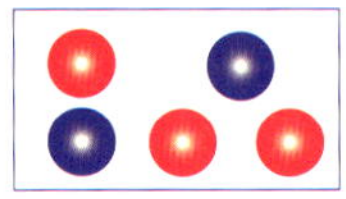	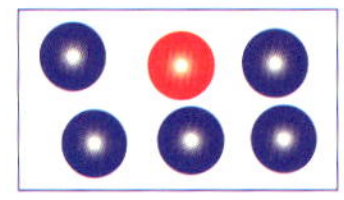
○	○	○	○
A	B	C	D

38. April is standing at the lookout. She is facing southeast.

What is April looking at?

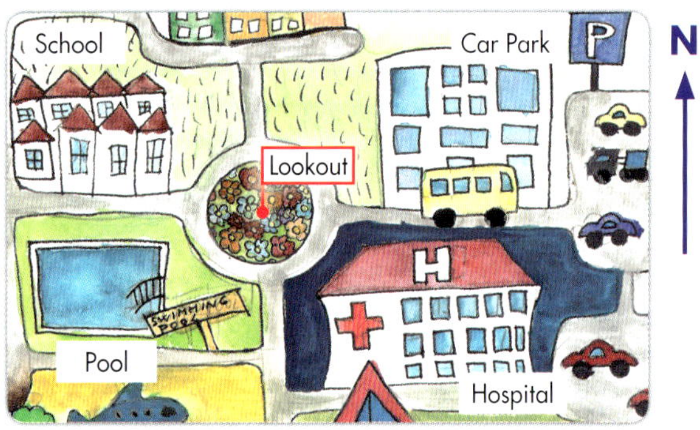

car park	school
○	○
A	B
swimming pool	**hospital**
○	○
C	D

39. Sarah is packing small boxes into a large box.

What is the greatest number of small boxes that will fit in the large box?

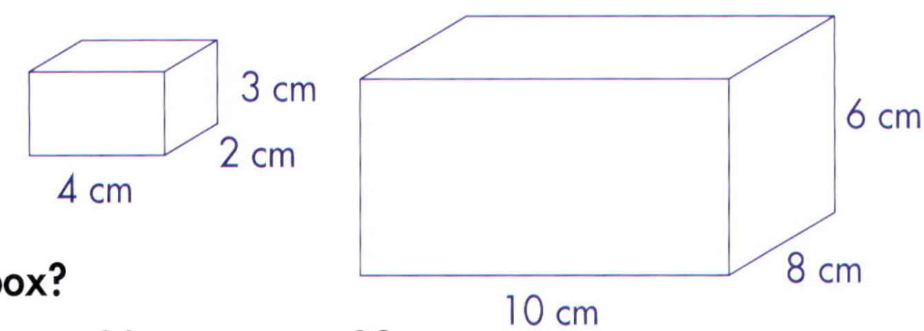

16	18	20	22
○	○	○	○
A	B	C	D

40. Here are two pictures of the same cube. Each face is a different colour.

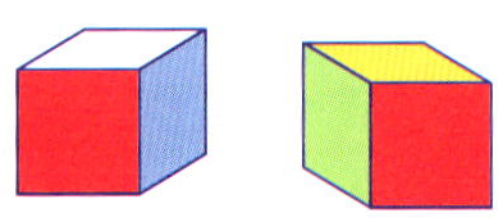

What colour could the face opposite the red face be?

white	green	yellow	purple
○	○	○	○
A	B	C	D

END OF TEST

Try this ANSWERS

Reading

Page

2 Single word

worst

2 Sequencing

various

3 Short answer

The author doesn't like school. They use negative words such as 'dreadful' and 'pain' to describe it.

7 Locating information

Holding

We have body parts made of keratin

Up to 250

8 Directly located information – character's motivation

Mum wants him to clean up instead

10 Connecting information

Seeing cartoons at the movies and on TV

She made short animations by scanning in her drawings

12 Making inferences

She can't remember anything

School students

13 Making inferences

People who donate to animal welfare groups

14 Making inferences

She was a strong, determined woman

admiration

16 Applied comprehension

A narrator

Ungrateful

17 Applied comprehension

The author wishes that money really did grow on trees

Marnie, Dreadful news, Loved one lost, My worst moment, Waiting

19 Visual literacy

Melting snow increases surface run off

giraffes will not feed at the same tree for a long time

Only the leaves are always poisonous

21 Sequencing

2 Dust particles create heat through friction

1 The particles within a nebula begin to rotate

4 Energy radiates out from the star

3 Helium is created

22 Sequencing

A transformer

It needs to have a lot of force to push the heavy turbines

23 Main idea

Investigators use evidence from the crime site to identify the criminal and solve the case.

25 Reasoning

Don't believe everything you see in advertising

26 Reasoning

Gorillas could live longer

28 Figurative language

alive

distant gun shots

29 Figurative language

He was concentrating on his work

The sound of the mice's teeth chewing at the rope

30 Punctuation and its purpose

To contain additional information

34 Practice reading test

1. To explain the circulatory system
2. To provide a definition
3. blood stops flowing
4. 2 The blood leaves the right ventricle

   4 The blood leaves via the left ventricle

   1 The blood travels through the vena cava

   3 Oxygenated blood returns to the heart

   5 The blood travels around the body
5. a cycle
6. frightened and reluctant
7. protective
8. her torch
9. He was nervous and a bit reluctant. He wanted to go back upstairs and not confront the burglar. He had to wipe his hands because they were sweaty. You get sweaty hands when you are nervous.

10. To show that she waits for Flynn

35 Practice reading test

11. The Butchers should sing their own songs
12. She is talking directly to the band
13. Lack of freedom
14. Not everyone has the same opinion
15. water, oxygen and light
16. draw the reader's attention to different information
17. Plastic shopping bags
18. Different categories of waste have different treatments methods
19. Biodegradable waste must be recycled

Writing

Various answers

Language Conventions

112 Spelling

1. ancient
2. body
3. wrapped
4. pyramids

113 Spelling

1. tropical
2. unusual
3. admitted
4. hopeful

113 Rule 1

1. reptile
2. backstroke
3. shape
4. grope

114 Rule 2

1. beady
2. brain
3. throat
4. venue

114 Rule 3

1. fullback
2. hammock
3. limerick
4. fleck

115 Rule 4

1. admitting
2. plugged
3. flatten
4. attention

115 Rule 5

1. amazement
2. shaking
3. slimy
4. priceless

116 Rule 6

1. bunnies
2. chimneys
3. enjoys
4. melodies

116 Rule 7

1. giraffes
2. strives
3. engulfs
4. chiefs
5. ourselves
6. relieve

117 Rule 8

1. blemishes
2. quenches
3. prefixes
4. indexes

117 Rule 9

1. retrieve
2. achieve
3. deceitful
4. hygiene
5. perceive

118 Rule 10

1. already
2. although
3. always
4. almost

118 Rule 11

1. switch
2. fetch
3. glitch
4. scratched

119 Silent letters

1. debt
2. whistle

119 AR or ER word endings

1. caterpillar
2. helicopter

119 EE or EA word endings

1. tweezers
2. increase

119 ION words

1. decision
2. division

120 GH words

1. enough
2. caught
3. breakthrough
4. daughter

120 OUS words

1. dangerous
2. adventurous

120 Commonly used words

choice
while
unusual
uncle

ocean

bicycle

would

suddenly

weather

favourite

125 Grammar

many

his

once until

most horrible

126 Homophones

They're

pause

126 Verb form

came

are going

126 Subject/verb agreement

jumps

pound

126 Pronoun referencing

them

127 Pronoun referencing

I your

127 Prepositions

by

with

127 Articles

a

an

127 Conjunctions

but

neither nor

By

128 More tips and tricks

among

hit

done

must have

133 Practice language conventions text

1. reflection
2. distance
3. laundry
4. bewitched
5. athletic
6. container
7. guess
8. engine
9. mechanic
10. Hopefully
11. Repaired

134 Practice language conventions test

12. diseases
13. Beware
14. signature
15. disappear
16. dangerously
17. tells
18. Dijon and Mustard
19. 3rd and 5th bubble
20. Samuel was preparing to play a trick on the Principal.

135 Practice language conventions test

21. Until Principal Wreck returns from the mental institution, the children are in control.
22. seen
23. in
24. people who study space
25. 2nd bubble
26. "How on earth am I going to do that?" I asked.

Numeracy

Page

143 Work it out!

54

4

11:00 am

144 Check it out!

4 metres

12×4

145 Try it out!

2

5

146 Don't be fooled!

Hall

147 Just imagine!

Half past 7

148 Guess!

12

149 Weed it out!

21

150 What could the answer be?

1500 mL

22

151 No problem!

1100

Checklists

152 Numbers and place value

30048

600 + 30 + 2

8752

153 Working with numbers

16

Subtract 17 from 83

154 Addition and subtraction

63

755

5, 6

155 Multiplication

48

6 × 6

170

156 Division

1203

13

8

157 Fractions and decimals

$\frac{3}{7}$

4 + 0.07

158 Money

$15.05

45 cents

159 Patterns

25

6.5 m

160 Measurement

Kilograms

500 mL

161 Time

4:15

7:51 am

162 Perimeter, area and volume

280 cm

15

163 Shapes

D

D

164 Objects

B

B

165 Location

Post office

166 Symmetry and transformation

D

A

167 Angles

D

B

168 Chance

Green

1 blue and 2 yellow marbles

169 Data

April

170 Numeracy practice test

1. A
2. 6
3. C
4. B
5. B
6. A

171 Numeracy practice test

7. C
8. D
9. B
10. A
11. 541
12. D

172 Numeracy practice test

13. A
14. C
15. A
16. C
17. 240

173 Numeracy practice test

18. A
19. B
20. C
21. D
22. B

174 Numeracy practice test

23. 10
24. B
25. 420
26. 69
27. A
28. C
29. D

175 Numeracy practice test

30. D
31. 24
32. B
33. A
34. D
35. B

176 Numeracy practice test

36. D
37. C
38. D
39. C
40. D